HIS
Royal
PLAN

JODIE LARSON

HIS Royal PLAN

CHAPTER
One

Luke

Something doesn't feel right. I know what I saw, but Gia's explanation makes sense. If I should be mad at anyone, it's my supposed best friend, Reid Mandrake. He's the back-stabber, trying to win her hand, knowing full well how deeply I care about her. Or how she feels about me.

It's there in every touch and caress. Each brush of our lips sends sparks through my body. I've never felt anything like this before. Her beauty, her wit, and her intelligence. Especially her sassy mouth, for more reasons than one. All of it rolled together into the perfect woman. Someone who will challenge me yet make me feel as if I could be myself.

There was a reason she flew all the way over to Lecara from America. Bryce and Connor Whittaker, my other two best friends, recognized our attraction instantly during Connor's bachelor party in Chicago. Was Reid so jealous that he didn't care?

I need to find Gia and tell her I believe her. How foolish could I be when the answers were all staring me right in the face? I know my mother is plotting against us. Why on earth would I believe anything she says?

My only hope is that I haven't ruined things with Gia.

There's more of a crowd now, people whispering and throwing glances my way. I'm sure Mother has stoked the embers, making sure it doesn't smolder and die.

"Lucien." Kiera's soft voice pulls me from my search.

I turn and greet her politely. She's not the woman I want to see right now. For whatever reason, she's been attached to me all night. The Wagner's have been closely tied to our family for years, so it's not surprising that Kiera is one of my oldest friends and someone I trust implicitly. Unlike Reid. It is a little strange she's still unmarried. She's more than beautiful enough with plenty of men wanting her attention. Yet, she clings to me as if we were together.

"Kiera, I'm sorry, but I'm a little busy right now."

She nods. "I heard. Your mother told me about the situation." She says the last word so quietly, like it was almost painful to utter.

My mother—the great Queen Marguerite. Beloved wife of my father, King Frederick, and adored by everyone. Only they don't know what she's really like behind closed doors. Everything is always carefully calculated and planned out. Nothing is left to chance, finding ulterior motives behind every move.

Why would she entrust this information to Kiera, who has nothing to do with this? "I appreciate your concern, but right now I need to speak with Ms. Hartley."

Kiera places a hand on my arm. I resist pulling away. Hers

is not the touch I want. "If you need anything, please know I'm here for you."

Without warning, she reaches up and embraces me tightly, pulling us so close there's barely any space between. I tense instantly, not sure what is going on. This whole night has turned into a clusterfuck. Gia and I were supposed to be happy, not end up in a fight about a misunderstanding. It's like everyone is working against us.

I gently pry her off me. "Thank you, Kiera. If you'll excuse me, please."

Without looking back, I continue my mission, not willing to stop until I find Gia.

"Lucien."

Fuck me.

I turn and come face-to-face with my mother. Once again her mask of indifference is firmly in place, never showing her hand.

"Not now, Mother. I'm trying to find Gia. I need to talk to her."

"That's what I'm here to tell you." Unease settles in my stomach. "Ms. Hartley left."

"She left?" No, that can't be right. I told her I needed a moment, not the whole night. Was I wrong in pushing her away to gather my thoughts, rather than working through the problem with her?

"She couldn't have."

Mother sighs and nods. "She has. A few minutes ago." She pauses. "With Mr. Mandrake."

Twice in the same night, I'm knocked off my feet.

She ran away with Reid?

No, that doesn't make sense. Her tears were real in the

bathroom. Her pain was splattered all over her face. Her pleas of understanding still echo in my ears.

She's either the greatest actress alive or someone is not being honest.

"I'm so sorry, my love. It appears her true colors have shown."

I swing my gaze to her, unable to feel anything.

Did I push her into his arms?

How could I have been so wrong?

Everything I know comes crashing down around my feet, leaving me without a shovel to dig myself out.

What am I going to do?

Someone is lying to me. I don't appreciate being played like a puppet.

Now I just need to figure out who.

CHAPTER
Two

Gia

"Ugh, no."

The drums pound a vicious beat in my head as the first rays of sunlight peek through the semi-closed curtains. Maybe it wouldn't be so bad if I had gotten an ounce of sleep, however, everything is working against me. Time. Space. Hell, the universe.

Last night was supposed to be amazing. Luke—aka Prince Lucien Alexander Frederick Claymore of Lecara—was going to make our relationship public. No more hiding in the shadows or secret meetings, wondering if we were always fated to be vacation flings or something more. Ever since he came into the bar in Chicago with his three best friends, my life hasn't been the same. He changed it for the better. Everything that was put into motion has happened for a reason.

And yet, it all fell apart and I don't know how to fix it.

I was supposed to be waking up in his arms. Instead, I'm

waking up still wearing the ball gown from last night in someone else's bed.

Someone who I'm still kind of pissed at and need to have a very lengthy—and loud—conversation with. Reid, Luke's best friend—or used to be before last night—was kind enough to bring me to his house since I had nowhere to go. Being forced to leave the gala was not something I planned on. And I didn't want to inconvenience the Whittaker family by stealing their driver to bring me back to their house. Besides, after the stunt Reid pulled last night and the gossip that quickly followed, who knows if I'm even allowed back there.

Part of me wants to close my eyes and never wake up. The other part wants to storm the palace and kick and scream until they let me in. One way or another, Luke will hear me out.

No sense lying in bed all day. I need to get to work on a plan.

Queen Marguerite will not win. I won't allow it.

Just the thought of Luke's mom churns whatever remnants are left in my stomach. I don't know what I did to piss her off, but she made it abundantly clear last night that I was not the girl for her son.

Luckily, she doesn't get to decide that.

First, I need to find a way to see Luke again. Groveling is not out of the question.

The cold floor sends a chill up my spine as I wander the strange house in search of some much-needed caffeine. If only it would freeze my brain and shut off my thoughts.

Why on earth did he kiss me? How could he do something like that to his best friend?

Before I leave this house, I will get my answers.

The enormous ball gown swishes around my feet as I walk into the kitchen.

"Hey," Reid says, already sitting at the breakfast bar with a steaming mug in hand.

"Hey." Dark circles rim his eyes, looking a little like death warmed over. I'm sure I'm not any better. "Did you get any sleep?"

He shakes his head. "Not a wink. You?"

I open a few cabinets before he points me in the right direction. "Same." The dark roast soothes my tired bones as I take a seat at the counter, leaving ample space between me and Reid. At least two cups of coffee are needed before I can even form coherent sentences to lay into this man.

He must sense it too, never once looking my way or attempting to start a conversation. Guilt and regret are written all over his face. Maybe I won't even need to lay into him as much as I think. It appears he's chewed his own ass all night.

No. His actions warrant a conversation.

Taking a deep breath, I twist the mug between my hands and sigh. "We need to talk about last night."

Reid visibly flinches. "I know. I've spent the whole night writing an apology in my head to you, to Luke, hell, to everyone. There's no excuse for my actions. I take full blame and responsibility for them."

"You're damn right you do." Anger creeps into my voice, though I try to tone it down. "How could you do that to me? To Luke? Do you have any idea what you've done? You basically served my head on a silver platter to Marguerite, giving her all the ammunition she needs to rid me from Luke's life."

Reid picks his head up, eyes rimmed red, to focus on me. "What are you talking about?"

"She hates me, been trying to find a way to get rid of me since I arrived. Your little stunt played right into her hand. I don't know all the details, but I'm willing to bet she's the one who alerted Luke to my supposed infidelity. Not to mention she kept shoving Kiera Wagner in my face all night."

"What does she have to do with it?" He draws his brows together.

Wait, does he not know? "Isn't she his soon-to-be wife? Aren't they betrothed?"

He laughs—actually laughs—at the notion. "No one has been betrothed in generations. Our government got rid of that rule decades ago, found it to be archaic and unnecessary. Not to mention enough royals threw fits about not being able to choose their partners. Stations and status are no longer required for marriage."

"So she lied to me," I say under my breath. She was feeding the seed of doubt in my head until it fully took over. What a bitch. If only I could have words with her, though it's highly unlikely I'll ever get close enough to tell her off. Not to mention I'll be banished from the country.

"To an extent."

What?

Reid stands to make another pot of coffee. "Kiera and Luke were childhood friends. Kiera's always had a crush on him, but he only looked at her as a sister. Of course, their parents always talked about joining their families together since Kiera came from noble stock and Luke being the spare heir. They had hoped a relationship would naturally form."

A million thoughts twist through my head as my heart is pinned in a vise. "Did they ever?"

Reid smiles. "Almost. Something got in the way before anything started."

I'm almost afraid to ask. "What?"

He pauses, leaving me in suspense. "Chicago."

If I wasn't already sitting, I would have fallen over. "He broke it off because of me?"

"Not exactly. She was ready to go after him, but he had no idea how she felt. After our return, he blew her off every time she called because he was so preoccupied with you, no one else would do."

A small part of me should take that as a compliment, but it does little good now. "I'm sure she's chomping at the bit with a helpful nudge from Marguerite."

"I wouldn't doubt it."

Something still bugs me. "If you knew how he felt about me after you returned, why did you keep trying to pursue me?"

Reid turns away, scrunching his shoulders as he retakes his seat. "I was jealous."

"I knew that much. How about a real answer?"

His normally clear brown eyes cloud over, showing his remorse over his actions. "Everyone always chooses Luke. They all flock around him, drawn to his name, his title. For once, I wanted to win the girl."

Unbelievable. "I'm not some prize to be won. I'm a human being with feelings and a choice. Do I think you're attractive? Of course. I'm not blind." His lips perk up slightly. "But there's no spark between us. I don't feel the butterflies in my stomach or the rush of blood every time you look at me."

Reid lets out a sigh, keeping his focus on the coffee mug. "I know. I could see it in your eyes every time you looked at him. And I knew you weren't after anything since we kept you in the dark about who he really was. Your attraction was genuine with no ulterior motives."

"Then you should have respected us and given your support instead of being a petulant child."

"I know." His voice is barely audible. "I feel awful for my actions. Is there any way you can forgive me?"

Taking a moment, I weigh all the options before me. Yes, he made an egregious error in judgment, but he's truly sorry for his actions. He's not placating me with words I want to hear. There's genuine emotion behind them.

However, the wound is still too fresh, the betrayal still raw in my mind.

"Probably, but not right now."

He nods sullenly. "I understand. I swear, I'll make it up to you. Both of you."

I don't know how he'll manage to pull it off, but at this point, I may need all the help I can get. Trying to get Luke to see his mother for who she really is could be difficult. I would never want to come between a mother and son, only this is war. Clearly, she thinks she's untouchable.

She's never messed with a girl from Chicago.

After helping him with the few dishes left in his sink, I make my way to the bedroom and find my phone on the floor next to the bed and power it up. I didn't want to talk to anyone after my sudden departure last night. Too afraid of what they would say. Probably shun me for being a whore, even though I'm not. The Whittakers probably have all my stuff packed up and sitting in the driveway as we speak—minus the clothes from Kendra's store. I'm sure she took those back.

I stare at the screen, waiting for it to show my fate. Finally I unlock the phone and my eyes widen at the number in the little red icon on the messages app.

Twenty-seven? I was expecting two or three, most of them saying to leave and never come back.

I tap the icon and hold back a smirk. Figures, the vast

majority of them are from Bryce. A few from Kendra. Nothing from Luke.

My heart aches in my chest, feeling the loss. Part of me hoped he would check in after needing space. Obviously, he needs more time.

I scroll through Bryce's messages, most of them touting the same words:

Bryce: Where are you?

Bryce: What happened?

Bryce: Gia, call me. I'm worried about you.

Bryce: This isn't funny anymore.

Bryce: Please, tell me you're alive.

Shit. I shouldn't worry him. He's been a true friend and in our corner from the beginning.

My fingers fly across the screen, trying to put out the raging fire.

Me: I'm alive. Don't send a search party out.

Three dots instantly appear. Jesus, was he sitting by his phone waiting?

Bryce: DO YOU KNOW HOW WORRIED I'VE BEEN?????

All caps. Yikes. That's not good.

Me: I'm sorry.

Bryce: Where are you??? I'll come get you.

Do I tell him? How pissed will he be?

Time to put my big girl pants on and face the music. Really, I don't have anything to be ashamed of or hide. Things were put into motion that I couldn't control. And if he can't understand the situation, I'll have to figure things out on my own.

I really hope he understands.

Me: At Reid's place.

And there it is. Silence.

He's mad. Or disappointed.

Probably both.

Bryce: On my way.

I can't tell if he's upset or not. This is why conversing about an important topic like this over text is never a good idea.

Too late now.

With my clutch in one hand and heels in the other, I make my way back to the kitchen, letting Reid know I have a ride home.

He hasn't moved from his spot at the counter, still staring at his coffee mug as if it had all the answers in the world.

"Bryce is picking me up," I say quietly.

Reid nods, acknowledging my announcement but not replying.

I hate to see him like this, so broken and beaten. However, he has no one to blame other than himself. This hailstorm is his doing. I don't know how he'll repair the damage, but he vows to make things right.

For both our sakes, I hope so.

The phone pings in my hand, letting me know of Bryce's arrival.

"Reid, I want you to know I still think of you as a friend, even though I'm pissed at you."

The chair screeches across the tiles as he stands and walks me to the door.

"Don't worry. I'm pissed at myself too." He swings the door open and I shiver as a cold breeze flutters across my bare arms. "Things will work out. I know it. You and Luke are the real deal."

A smile cracks his face, feeling my own start to pull at my lips.

"Thanks."

I lean over and wrap my arms around him, sending some encouragement his way. He's not a bad guy. Only misguided.

Lights flash off to the side, whipping my head around so fast stars appear in front of my eyes. What the fuck?

The car parked across the street speeds away as Bryce pulls up in front of Reid's house.

Great. A well-timed photo of me walking out in last night's dress, hugging the man who sent the gala into a frenzy and hurt their beloved prince.

Fuck. My. Life.

CHAPTER
Three

Gia

Bryce doesn't utter a word the entire way back to his house. You could practically cut the tension with a knife. This isn't good. Not even a little bit. If I lose him, I'll have nothing left to keep me here. I can't imagine Kendra is willing to hear me out.

"Bryce, please, say something." A tear threatens to fall, but I hold it back, waiting to see if he's going to hand out a judgment or fight for my cause.

With his eyes still fixed on the road, he sighs heavily, his shoulders slumping forward slightly. "Do you have any idea how worried I was last night? I didn't know if you were in an accident or if you'd run away or worse." His voice wavers, full of the emotion he's been holding back. The car jerks to the side before getting thrown into park. Bryce reaches over and drags me into a soul-crushing embrace. "You're not allowed to do that again."

This time I let the tears flow freely. His concern eases some of the pain and worry from deep within as I squeeze him tight.

"I was so afraid you'd never speak to me again."

He laughs and kisses the side of my head. "Hate to break it to you, but you're stuck with me for life. We're family."

It's amazing how quickly and almost seamlessly I've glided into his family. Both his parents dote on me like one of their own, including me in all family functions. Connor and Kendra treat me like everyone else.

Though Kendra might not feel the same anymore.

I pull back and wipe the back of my hand across my cheeks. "Kendra may not agree."

His frown tells me the answer before I even ask. "She will. Give it time."

Something I don't have.

Bryce pulls back onto the road and before long, the Whittaker Manor comes into view. Still as impressive as when I first saw it. Old-world architecture you'd never find in Chicago. History practically clings to every wall, through the paintings and antiquated fixtures and furnishings.

Yet, it feels every bit like my home, just like my tiny one-bedroom apartment.

George greets us at the garage as Bryce pulls in. "Good morning, Mr. Whittaker, Gia." He tips his hat and backs the luxury black town car out, which means he's either picking someone up or someone is getting ready to leave. Part of me was hoping no one would be home to witness my walk of shame. The once illustrious silver dress is now dirty at the hem and wrinkled beyond repair. I was hoping I could keep it for a future engagement, but at this rate, it'll need to be burned.

Bryce slings an arm around my shoulder and guides me inside. "Don't worry. Everything will be fine."

Easy for him to say. He didn't create a monstrous

scandal, leaving him the talk of the town. Hopefully not the world.

Still carrying my heels, I tiptoe against the cool floor, praying no one comes out and I can lock myself in my room until everyone has moved on from this disaster.

Kendra turns a corner, her eyes narrowing at me as she gets closer.

Shit. No such luck.

Bryce stands in front, shielding me from her glare. "Kendra, listen."

She shoves him out of the way and stands toe to toe with me. Pain flashes across her face. She was an innocent victim in this mess. Technically so was I, but no one will see it that way.

"How could you?" The cracks in her voice are like a knife stabbing me in the lungs, taking away my breath with each strike.

"I-I didn't. I swear. Kendra, please listen."

She holds up a hand, halting my progress. "There's nothing you could say that I'll believe. I asked you time and again if there was something going on with Reid. You encouraged me to go for him, and then you do this?"

Bryce steps to my side, squaring his shoulders as if ready for a fight. "She didn't do anything, Kendra. This was all Reid. You know as well as I do how much she cares for Luke. Why on earth wouldn't you believe her?"

The pain and betrayal shadow her eyes. "People say one thing and do another. It's why people cheat. They're never satisfied with what they have, always wanting more." She swings her icy gaze to me, chilling me from head to toe. "And you've been stringing them both along for weeks. Reid during the day and Luke at night."

I can't believe she basically called me a whore. "Kendra, I swear upon everything holy and sacred that I have *zero* interest in Reid. He's a friend. Nothing more."

For a moment, I think I may have gotten through to her. She types something on her phone, scrolling a bit before turning it to me.

All the blood drains from my face as I stare at the picture taken less than an hour ago. My arms around Reid on his doorstep, wearing this wrinkled dress, hair messed up like I had sex all night. All of it with the caption "Jilted Prince Made A Fool By American Woman."

No. No. No. No. No. NO!

Snatching the phone from her hand, I scroll and read the article, finding pictures of me and Luke kissing at the gala, us dancing together, then Reid and I dancing, his incredibly stupid kiss, us leaving, and then a smaller one of the main article picture, only with my look of shock at the camera.

"Nothing about this is right." How could they make up such an elaborate story? Better yet, how did they get all these small details? No one knew about our secret dates or late-night phone calls.

Except one who could easily get access to everything she wants because of her power.

"How could she do this to me?" I whisper, a tear falling down my cheek.

Kendra yanks the phone from my grasp before I drop it. "Who? You have no one to blame but yourself. It's all there in the pictures, Gia."

"I know it sounds like I'm making excuses, but I'm not. Someone is out to get me, create doubt and deceive Luke about who I am."

Bryce places a hand on my arm. "Who would do such a thing?"

Kendra scoffs. "Don't fall for her lies, dear brother. You're just as in love with her as the other two fools. I won't see you get caught up in this either." She glances at her watch. "And now I'm late for a meeting. If you'll excuse me."

She brushes past us, not interested in anything I have to say. Not that I blame her. If the tables were turned, I'd be just as upset.

Not true. I'd hear her out but take a day to process her words and fact check the events. Not believe the information found on some seedy gossip website whose paychecks rely on the misfortune of others.

Bryce wraps his arm around my shoulders and helps me to my room. "I'll talk to her."

I shake my head. "Don't. It'll only make things worse. She needs a day to cool off before she can listen to reason."

He sets me down on the edge of my bed, taking the spot next to me. "Luckily for you, I don't need a day."

The last thing I want to do is drag Bryce into this mess, especially when I don't have all the answers. I can only make an educated guess as to who's behind this morning's photos. But without real proof, no one would believe me. Why would their beloved queen go after an American woman? Knowing my luck, someone would find out what I said and I'd be tried for treason and banished from the country.

"I appreciate it, Bryce. I really do. But I need to get a few facts first before I can say anything."

He nods in understanding. "Whenever you're ready, I'm here to discuss Marguerite's utter hatred for you."

Before I have the chance to ask him what he means, he

kisses the side of my head and walks out the door, leaving me with more questions than answers.

How does he know? Did Luke confide in him about his suspicions? Or did he overhear something at the gala last night?

I need to get to the bottom of this.

But first, a hot, steamy shower.

Which did nothing to help clear the fog from my thoughts or give me any good ideas on how to start fixing this mess.

With Kendra basically not speaking to me and still no word from Luke, I'm at a loss. I can't talk to Reid after this morning's incident because that will make everything worse. And I don't want to drag Bryce into anything he doesn't need to be in.

Looking around the luxurious room, one thing is painfully clear. Until this all blows over and the truth is exposed, I won't be able to stay here. I can't face Miriam and Thomas, nor do I want to avoid Kendra every time I walk around the house. They shouldn't be uncomfortable in their own home. The easiest solution is to eliminate the problem: me.

I grab the suitcase out of the closet and start packing it with the clothes I brought from Chicago, leaving the high-end fashion items in the closet. My phone rings on the bedside table and I practically twist my ankle sprinting to check the caller ID.

"Hey, Ang." Not the person I was hoping for, but still a pleasant surprise.

"Girl, what in the hell is going on over there? Your face is splashed all over the internet right now."

I cringe and fall back on the plush comforter. Man, I'm going to miss this. "Don't remind me. It's a mess and I don't know how to fix it."

"I'm sure you'll think of something. You're the best problem solver I know. Besides, that handsome prince of yours has to know how you feel about him."

Angie and Callie, my two best friends from back home, are the only ones who know the full story—except for the events of last night. After the disastrous garden party, they got an earful of Marguerite's disgust of me. But that was the only thing they got out of me. The dessert party afterward in Luke's bedroom was never mentioned. Our moments together will stay private for as long as possible. I'm not about to willingly give anyone tabloid fodder.

"He's sort of not speaking to me currently. And Kendra is furious. You should have seen her face when I got back home."

Angie pauses. "What on earth were you thinking spending the night at Reid's? If the situation was reversed, I'd react the same way."

I blow out a breath. "I know. I wasn't thinking. Marguerite basically told me that Luke is betrothed and I should just leave. Then she made sure I noticed every time Luke and Kiera were together, dancing or embracing or laughing at something."

"Wait, who's Kiera?"

"The girl he's supposedly engaged to, though Reid was quick to rebut that info, saying they got rid of betrothals years ago."

"And you trust him?" she says skeptically.

"He has no reason to lie about it. If he was trying to make a move, he would have gone along with the fabrication rather than contradict it."

"True." Her voice softens. "I'm so sorry. Does this change your plans? Please tell me you're not coming home."

I pull at the hem of my shirt. "I-I don't know yet."

"Well, I refuse to let you board that plane until you clear

things up, so if you're entertaining that thought, stop it right now. I won't allow it."

I laugh at her absurdity. As if she has any say on what I do. Even though she's right. There's no way I can leave right now. Not when things are messed up. There was a reason I came here, a reason these four guys stepped into my bar a couple months ago. And no amount of scheming from his evil mother will stop me.

"Don't worry, I'm staying. Though probably not here. I won't subject the Whittakers to any of this madness. Not to mention make things uncomfortable in their own house."

"So what are you going to do?"

Holding the phone against my shoulder, I zip up the suitcase and set it on the floor. "Not sure yet. Maybe find a hotel for a couple days to start. Then go from there."

I do a final check in the room, making sure I have all the essentials. If I'm going to have a hotel stay, money will be limited and I'd rather not buy two of something I already have.

"You do you, boo. I'd say call me later, but I'll be working and then passing out. Shoot me a message sometime soon."

"Will do."

We say our goodbyes and I look around the room, saying a silent goodbye to it as well.

With George occupied taking Kendra somewhere and no idea where Bryce is, I use the opportunity to start walking down the road, mindful of any oncoming cars. I don't want to put George in a horrible position either, forcing him to keep a secret on my whereabouts. Maybe later tonight, once I have things situated, I'll let Bryce know where I am. Until then, he can think I'm wallowing in grief in my room.

Once I get a decent cell signal, I call for a taxi and give them the general location, with the help of a dilapidated farm sign at the intersection. I try to stay out of sight, in case anyone comes looking for me. No one's called my phone yet, so I'm hoping to stay under the radar for a bit longer.

The white car pulls up to the side of the road and I'm greeted by a friendly male.

"Running away from something, miss?"

I climb into the back seat and flash a fake smile. "Not at all." God, I hope he doesn't pay attention to the tabloids. The last thing I want to do is answer questions about the situation.

Luckily, the ride to town was smooth, making small talk about the weather and what I've enjoyed so far on my trip. He drops me off at one of the cheaper hotels he recommended. I give my thanks—and a large tip—and exit the car, thankful this first part is over. Bryce started calling me as we got into town, so I had to shut off the phone because I couldn't keep ignoring it.

The street corner looks familiar as I spin in a small circle, looking at the various shops and buildings. That's right, we came here not too long ago. The Bull & Boar Pub is across the street, bringing back memories of Luke surprising me while we pretended not to care about each other. I wonder if Matt still wants to hire me.

Dragging my suitcase behind me, I open the door and cringe at the dumb bell. Hopefully if I get hired, I'll learn to tune it out.

Matt stands behind the bar, polishing a rack of steaming hot glasses before placing them on their shelves.

"Gia, right?" He remembered my name.

"Yeah, hi Matt." I take a seat at the bar and slump on my elbows. "Still have that job opening for me?"

He smirks and slides a full mug of beer my way. "Offer still stands if you want it."

I stall and take a drink, waiting for the cool liquid to loosen my muscles. After the events of the last twenty-four hours, my only plans for the night should be to get absolutely blasted drunk.

"Definitely. How soon do you need me?"

He chuckles as I set the empty mug down, only to be greeted by another full one. "Is tonight too soon?"

Well, so much for drinking my cares away. "Sounds good to me."

Matt looks over the bar, his brows drawn together. "You always bring a suitcase with you?"

My laugh sounds hollow, not anything like it should. "Only when I'm between places."

"Been there before." He gives a sympathetic smile and waves me down the hall. "Follow me."

We head out the back entrance and up the two flights of wooden stairs to the top floor of the building. Matt fishes out his keys and unlocks the door, swinging it open with a flourish.

A little dusty but tidy and well put together. Some new curtains, maybe some furniture covers and blankets and this could be cute. It reminds me of my apartment back in Chicago.

I turn in a circle, getting the full view. "How much?"

"We'll work something out." Matt smiles and shows me the modest bedroom, bathroom, and kitchen. "This space usually sits empty, so it'll be nice to have someone in here again. Not to mention if we get slammed, I have the backup bartender handy."

"Ah, so that's your plan," I say with a laugh. This feels right. Almost like I'm supposed to be here. "Are you sure about this? We barely know each other and you're offering me this job and apartment to rent."

Leaning against the doorjamb, he crosses his arms over his broad chest. "You look lost. People come to bars to find themselves. Figured this kills two birds with one stone."

Once again, I choke back tears for the millionth time today. The generosity and kindness everyone in Lecara has shown me absolutely blows me away. Well, almost everyone.

"Besides, no one will bother you here, in case you need to hide away."

"Oh," I say, looking at the floor. "So you know."

Matt nods. "I don't tend to get involved in gossip or bother myself with the royal family. However, I saw you with the prince before everything hit the press. I also saw you with the other guy. There's no doubt in my mind which one has your eye. The prince has been coming here for years because he can be himself without the press hanging around. Girls always try to get his attention, but he never gives it to them. You were different. Anyone could see you two clearly have deep feelings for each other."

A lump forms in my throat as his words sink in. We tried so hard to hide it from everyone, yet Matt saw it so easily. Marguerite probably had spies following us and reported what they saw, feeding her plot against me for whatever imaginary crime I committed.

"He may not feel the same way anymore."

Matt places a hand on my shoulder, giving it a light squeeze. "He will. I have a feeling about you two."

Okay, enough of this conversation. "What time do you want me downstairs? And what should I wear?"

He waves a hand up and down his body with a smirk. "You have jeans and a shirt?"

"Now you're talking my language."

Pausing at the door, Matt turns to face me. "Come down about six o'clock and I'll show you the basics, but I have a feeling you'll be just fine."

Once he's gone, I drag my suitcase to the bedroom, looking

over my new surroundings. Not as fancy as the Whittakers, but it's better than staying in some seedy motel. I check the bathroom and find it stocked with a few towels and toiletries. There's even a stacked washer and dryer tucked in a closet by the kitchen. Perfect. The less I need to go out, the better. I gather up the towels and sheets and throw them in there for good measure.

I take note of the few items I need to get—mostly food—and busy myself to organizing my bedroom. This is what I needed. A distraction.

Though not a complete one. My mind still wanders to Luke, wondering if he hates me or not. Or how far his mother's poison runs. I can picture her sitting on her throne, cackling over her victory in breaking us apart.

Fuck that. She messed with the wrong girl.

After making the bed and folding the towels, I throw my skinny jeans and favorite T-shirt on and head down early. No sense sitting around here alone with my thoughts when there's a bar downstairs.

Besides, alcohol fixes everything.

CHAPTER
Four

Luke

I stare out the window, watching the sun climb higher in the morning sky. Such a magical hour, when the stars disappear and the veiled darkness comes to light, chasing away any lingering shadows of the night.

Yet they taunt me with the deceit and lies of last night, reminding me of a betrayal so egregious my blood still simmers after so many hours. The only question that remains is who the ultimate culprit is.

The lack of sleep leaves my head aching, as well as my muscles after a restless night. Constantly going over the events until they practically made me dizzy, trying to pinpoint where everything went wrong. Mother has not shied away from her disdain of Gia, but could she be so heartless as to destroy the happiness of her son?

Then there's Gia, my sweet angel. Her actions and words over the last few weeks contradict the charges from my mother against her. Still, I can't get the image of her lips pressed against Reid's out of my mind. Those petal-soft lips belong to me. I can still feel them against my own, traveling across my body as we get lost in each other. Now they're tainted, ruined. The scene is burned against my eyelids every time I close them. The fissure on my heart widens as it replays over and over.

No one knows more than I do that not everything is as it seems. Appearances can be false, especially when they fit into someone else's plan.

Like my mother's.

Or Reid's.

I grit my teeth, trying not to grind them into dust. His betrayal hurts the most. My best friend, the one who encouraged me time after time to follow my dreams, never letting my title bring me down. And the one time I need him and his blessing, he turns around and stabs me in the back. What Gia and I have is like nothing I've ever experienced. He knows it and still couldn't help himself from taking what isn't his.

I mentally make a list of everyone I need to confront. And since it's Sunday, no better time than the present to approach the number one suspect on my list.

Feeling more like myself after a long, hot shower, I walk into the dining hall where both my parents are seated at the head of the table, not speaking—as normal—while eating their breakfast. Nick, my older brother, is nowhere to be seen, which is highly unusual. After his strange comments last night about wanting to do more than he's allowed, I wonder what's going on with him. Living for crown and country has been his life, one he's proud of. What's changed?

Mother glances up, displaying her saccharine smile as I take my seat. "Lucien, darling. You're looking well this morning, all things considered."

Wow, doesn't even hesitate to dig right in before I've had my morning coffee. Looks like she wants to throw down right away. Okay, let's play.

"Looks can be deceiving. Sort of like your false well wishes."

Father doesn't even look up from his paperwork as she gasps dramatically. "Why would you say such a thing? You know I only have your best interests at heart."

I thank the server as I take a sip of the freshly poured coffee. "Really Mother? There are no cameras to pose before or reporters to hear your double-edged sentiments."

Her cup clangs against the porcelain saucer, echoing throughout the hall. "Is that how you speak to me?"

"It is when you've been lying to me."

She slides her mask of indifference on, once again hiding her true feelings. "Nothing I did last night was false. Ms. Hartley, however, was the one who made a fool out of you, kissing Mr. Mandrake so publicly after spending so much time dancing with you." Her stone demeanor cracks a little as the corners of her lips turn up. "I believe you're projecting your anger on the wrong person, darling."

I turn to my father, still engrossed in his own world. How can he sit there and be so oblivious to his surroundings? Or not have an opinion on the matter at hand?

Clenching my fists beneath the table, I tamp the slowly simmering anger down. "Do you deny any sort of plotting then?"

A server appears, clearing the place settings before quickly retreating, knowing it's a conversation they shouldn't hear. "I have done nothing other than point out the truth."

"Your *truth* is based on your opinion. Do you not care about my feelings? What do you have against Gia in the first place? She's done nothing to you, yet you take pleasure in pointing out all her flaws."

"Flaws?" she scoffs. "If it were merely flaws, we wouldn't be having this conversation. Instead, she has been gallivanting about with other men behind your back. Then as soon as you come into the picture, she's back in your arms, waiting to strike."

Has she lost it? "You know she had no idea who I really was until Connor's wedding. How could you possibly think she has ulterior motives?"

She picks up her phone and quickly spins it my way.

What the fuck?

Gia and Reid. Front page of some gossip website.

In an intimate embrace on the front steps of his house.

Only this was taken within the hour.

No, this can't be right.

More pictures appear as I read on, ones of the two of us gazing into each other's eyes, kissing on the dance floor. Then pictures of Gia and Reid and their kiss. Them leaving together. And Gia's shocked expression as she stares into the camera from this morning. Still wearing last night's dress with her shoes in hand, hair messed up like she'd been rolling around all night.

Red creeps into my vision. No, this can't be true. There's no way my best friend and the woman of my affection would sneak around behind my back.

Mother places her cold hand on top of mine, her sad smile fueling my anger. "I'm so sorry, my dear. It's best you know the truth about her before things got too far."

The loud screech of the chair startles her as I toss the napkin on the table. "Excuse me."

I can practically feel her smugness as I walk away and pull my phone out, sending David—my personal driver—a text to meet me in five minutes.

After changing into a pair of jeans and a sweater, the black town car pulls up to the front entrance of my small cottage on the palace estate. If I'm going to do some investigating into these allegations, I need to blend in and not draw attention.

"Where to, Your Highness?"

I push the glasses up my nose before meeting David's eyes in the rearview mirror. "Mr. Mandrake's house, as quickly and quietly as you can. Try to lose any paparazzi if possible."

Gia's pleas echo in my ears the whole ride over. It killed me to see her tears, feel her pain as I walked away. I've never seen her look so defeated, even when we parted in Chicago, not knowing if we'd ever see each other again.

Am I letting my personal feelings toward her cloud my judgment? Could I have turned a blind eye to what was going on around me, ignoring the signs of her deception?

The one thing she's always been is honest. I have no reason to disbelieve her now.

After taking a few side streets to lose a car or two, David drops me off at Reid's house. Luckily the street is quiet as I exit the car, taking long strides straight to his front door. I knock once before barging inside. Reid's surprised expression is quickly knocked off his face as my right fist connects with his nose, sending blood dripping to the floor.

"You son of a bitch!" I swing again, ignoring the blinding pain in my hand as Reid drops to the ground, his left eye instantly swelling. I hover over him, my breath barely able to keep up as I stare him down. "How could you do this?"

Blood tinges the back of his hand as he wipes his nose. "I'm sorry."

His apology isn't enough. Does he not realize the damage he's caused? The hurt he unnecessarily placed on two innocent people?

"Not yet, but you will be."

I grab him by the shirt collar, dragging him to his feet with my arm cocked back, ready to strike.

"Do what you need to do. It's nothing less than I deserve."

His defeated tone and stare give me pause, taking in the scene with clear eyes. Even with everything that's happened, Reid is still my best friend and deserves the chance to explain himself without needing to be sent to the hospital for it.

Lowering my arms, he stumbles back slightly as I release my grip and walk to the kitchen to grab a paper towel, giving it to Reid as he takes a seat at the counter.

"Thanks," he mutters, pinching the bridge of his nose and tilting his head back.

I keep my distance, putting a chair between us as I join him at the counter. "Talk."

He turns slightly, squinting through one eye before taking a deep breath. "There's no excuse for my actions. I could say I was under the influence or the full moon made me do it, but it wouldn't be enough. Yes, I had too much to drink, which lowered my inhibitions and I showed poor judgment. But really, I wasn't thinking. Jealousy drove me mad because I wanted her too." My jaw tics as he finally admits the truth I've suspected all along. "I wanted her the moment we saw her in Chicago. And like always, she was drawn to you. I was so sick and tired of coming in second place. When she kept accepting my lunch dates, I thought for a brief moment that maybe she liked me too. Even though I knew how she felt about you and vice versa. It didn't matter."

I clench my fists and close my eyes, tamping down the anger brewing inside. "You selfish asshole. I was your best friend. How could you do something like that to me? Of all people, you know how hard it is to be myself around others. For the first time in my life, I had something real. She saw me, before she knew anything of my background. And you didn't care."

Reid hangs his head, trying to hide his shame behind the bloodied paper towel. "Like I said, I have no excuse. I really, truly am sorry. If there's any way I can make it up to you, I will. Anything."

Even though I want to pummel his face in, our lifelong friendship reminds me that he's human and made a mistake. It doesn't mean I have to forgive him right away.

"Right now, I need you to tell me everything that happened last night after you two left."

He draws his brows together as best he can. "What are you talking about?"

Does he not know? Or is he really that obtuse to think I wouldn't find out?

Dragging my phone from my back pocket, I find the website and hold it out for him to see.

I don't know what I was expecting, but shock was not it. "What the fuck?" He tries to scroll down to read the article and finally pushes it away. "Those are blatant lies. Who gave them this information?"

"I'd like to know the same thing," I say, tucking my phone away. There's no dishonesty in his eye. "Tell me if anything happened last night between you."

He shakes his head, though stops to grip the edge of the counter. "Nothing, I swear. She slept in my bed and I stayed on the couch."

His normally tidy living room is hardly recognizable. Blankets and pillows heaped on the furniture while coffee mugs and beer bottles litter the end tables. Loose sheets of paper lie scattered across the floor, some with writing, others completely blank.

"This is all from last night?"

Reid looks away. "Most of it. The beer bottles are over the last few nights. Everything else is within the last few hours." I pick up a piece of paper and start to read, realizing it's an apology letter addressed to me. "I was trying to work out how to explain this all to you and couldn't get the words right. I know I don't deserve your forgiveness, but I'd like to try anyway."

"What did Gia say this morning?" I ask, changing the subject.

He shrugs. "She slept about as well as I did, which was not at all. She's convinced your mom hates her and is behind this whole plot."

She's not the only one. The more stones I overturn, the more it becomes clear who the deceiver is. Guilt seeps in with this new realization. I'm just as much to blame for this mess as Reid. Why did I believe anything my mother said? I've known for weeks she disapproves of our relationship, but I never thought she'd do anything like this.

I get up and grab a bag of frozen vegetables and toss them to Reid. "Put this on your eye before it completely swells shut."

"Thanks." He catches it and lets out a hiss as the bag covers half his face. "Why does your mom hate Gia?"

"That is the question of the day. I wish I knew."

"And what's up with Kiera? Gia was under the impression you two were engaged."

I jerk my head back. "What? Why on earth would she think that."

He tilts his head. "Take a wild guess."

Right. The Evil Queen.

"What did you say?"

He flips the bag over, closing his good eye in relief. "I told her she was a close family friend and how Kiera's always had a crush on you, even though you never returned the feelings." Reid wipes his nose, checking for any residual blood. "I also mentioned you were about to entertain a relationship with Kiera, only one thing stopped you… and that was her."

I smile as I remember the day. Kiera and her father stopped by the palace, at the beckoning of my mother. We sat for afternoon tea and it was mentioned more than once by both our parents what a cute couple we could be. Kiera, dressed in her nicest garden dress, blushed like a schoolgirl as she looked for confirmation from me.

Then Gia popped into my head, remembering our night together and the time we spent on the Willis Tower overlooking Chicago, making me feel as if I was on top of the world with her in my arms. And I was. Nothing had ever felt more natural.

Another glance at Kiera only confirmed I couldn't go along with it. I won't string someone along just to fulfill an obligation.

Turning my attention back to Reid, I hold out my hand. "Sorry about your face."

He tentatively shakes it. "Sorry about last night."

"I'm still not forgiving your actions."

He nods. "Understood. Maybe one day?"

"Maybe." I stand and push the chair back in. "You might want to get your nose and eye checked."

Reid tries to laugh but flinches at the pain. "Probably."

I'm halfway to the front door when it bursts open, slamming violently against the wall. Bryce barrels into the room, his eyes frantically looking for something. Or someone.

"Is she here?"

Reid and I look to each other. "Who?"

"Gia," he says, completely out of breath.

Every hair stands on end as dread crawls through my body. "What's going on?"

Bryce closes his eyes and shakily inhales. "She's not at the house. I can't find her anywhere." Fear flashes in his eyes. "Luke, she's gone."

CHAPTER
Five

Luke

"**G**one? What do you mean she's gone?"

The three of us go to the living room, tossing the blankets on the floor. Bryce keeps checking his phone as if it will give him a different answer from the few seconds previously.

"I mean, she's not at the house anymore. No one knows where she is. None of the housekeepers have seen her and George was driving Kendra to town, so he doesn't know where she is either. It's like she's disappeared."

No, it can't be. Gia's not the sort of girl to run away from a situation. She has more grit than any other woman I know. Something's not right.

"Where could she have gone? I doubt she would have walked to town, especially if she was carrying something. Have you searched her room yet?" I ask, trying to keep my knee from bouncing too much. Even though Gia can take care of herself, a lot can happen to a woman out alone, regardless of the time of day. And if she was in the countryside with hardly any traffic, anything is possible.

It feels like a rock has lodged itself in the pit of my stomach, churning up bile and unease.

"Let's not get ahead of ourselves," Reid says, tossing the now-melted bag of vegetables on the table. "Maybe she needed to cool off, gain some perspective."

For the first time, Bryce looks over to Reid and frowns. "What happened to your face?"

With half of it swollen and bruised, he looks like he went several rounds with a professional boxer. A part of me feels bad for messing him up. Then I remember his lips on Gia and those thoughts get overruled.

"Nothing," we say at the same time.

Bryce nods, choosing not to say anything else. Smart man.

I stand up and start pacing behind the couch. "Let's retrace her steps. She left the gala, came here and spent the night." I barely get the words out through gritted teeth. Reid looks away, avoiding any judgment from his two friends. "Then you pick her up." Bryce nods. "And then what?"

"Kendra confronted us in the hallway, showing us the tabloid blowing everything out of proportion." Jesus, how many people have seen that article already? "She had a few choice words." He looks to me and bites his bottom lip. I nod, encouraging him to continue. "Basically called her a whore and then left. I brought Gia to her room and left her there, figured she could use some alone time or a nap because she looked like death walking. After an hour, I went to check on her and she wasn't there. I've asked everyone I know and no one has seen or heard from her. Do you think she went home?"

It's a possibility, not one I'm inclined to entertain right now. "Let's go back to your house and see if we can find any clues on where she went."

The two of them nod as we walk out the front door and climb into Bryce's car, speeding down the road as fast as we can.

"You're not going to get blood all over the car, are you?" he asks, glancing at Reid in the rearview mirror.

"Fuck off," he says, wiping his nose with a clean tissue.

I smirk, glad we're back to the same old banter again. At least for a little while. It's a good distraction, stopping the "what if" scenarios from constantly playing.

She has to be okay. I won't allow any other scenario to occupy my thoughts.

The car skids to a stop on the gravel drive in front of the Whittaker Manor. The three of us pile out quickly, taking the front steps two at a time, blowing past servants and making a beeline for her room.

On first inspection, everything appears normal. Bed neatly made, nothing overturned, clothes still in the closet.

Wait.

I slide the hangers across the rod, noting it's only the things Kendra and I bought for her. I run to the dresser, the drawers easily sliding with a tug. Empty. No jeans or shirts. No lingerie. No evidence that she ever occupied the room.

"The bathroom's been cleared out," Bryce calls from the open door.

"So has her dresser," I say, slamming the drawers shut.

"I can't find her suitcase anywhere," Reid says.

Fuck! She is gone.

I walk over to the bed and sit on the edge, hanging my head between my knees. This can't be happening.

"I hate to say it," Bryce starts but I shoot him a chilling glance, stopping him from completing that sentence.

Grabbing my phone, I pull up the airline she flew in on, checking to see if they have any upcoming flights back to the U.S. Since her ticket was open-ended, she could fly back whenever she feels like it.

I really hoped she'd never want to use it. I hope I'm still right.

"We need to get to the airport," I say, shoving my phone back in my pocket. "There's a flight to the U.S. leaving in an hour. If we hurry, we might catch it."

Both of them nod as we race through the house, ignoring everything as we climb into Bryce's car and speed away, kicking up dirt and gravel as the tires spin against their will.

She can't leave. I was such a fool to believe anything my mother said. Why did I let her manipulate me so easily? Was I really that insecure about Gia leaving?

I stare out the passenger window, barely registering the scenery as it whips by.

"We'll find her," Reid says. "And everything will be all right."

I glance over my shoulder and nod, unable to form any words at the moment. Too many emotions are clogging my throat. Too many things I left unsaid.

The closer we get to the airport, the harder my heart beats in my chest. What if we're too late? What if she took another flight and she's already over the Atlantic?

No. I won't entertain that thought, refuse to deem it a possibility. We will find her and I'll apologize profusely for my reprehensible behavior.

After arguing with security and playing my royalty card, we sprint through the corridors, dodging people while receiving several obscene gestures and comments.

"Here, this one," Bryce says, taking a sharp right. Just our luck, the gate is all the way at the end of the hall. Everything inside of me aches and burns, as if all my organs are ready to implode.

"Oh no," Reid says, slowing down slightly.

The gate is empty, except a lone attendant typing at the computer desk. She looks up as the three of us slam our hands down on the counter.

"Hello. Anything I can help you with?"

I take a shaking breath and swallow hard, proving to be more of a chore with my dry, scratchy throat.

"The flight to New York. Has it left yet?"

Her eyes soften as she frowns. "Unfortunately it just departed." She points to the window showing the massive plane taxiing away from the gate. "Did you need to rebook your flight?"

I slump against the counter, cradling my head in my hands. We're too late. Gia's gone.

The only person to ever see me for me is gone because I didn't have enough faith in her, listening to the lies, knowing in my heart she'd never do anything to hurt me. You don't cross an ocean for someone you might like. There was a connection between us.

"Sir?"

Without acknowledging her question, I turn and walk away.

"Uh, no, thank you," Bryce says before catching up to me. Reid takes the other side, both flanking me like my own personal protection.

Not a word is spoken. No need to. They know nothing can bring her back.

Reid is the first to break the silence once we're in the car.

"Luke, I'm really sorry. I swear I didn't mean for any of this to happen."

I keep my gaze out the window. There must be something I can do. This isn't the end of us. I won't accept it.

I'm not sure how long we drive around but by the time Bryce parks the car, night has started to fall with the first few stars gleaming in the sky. I stare at the Bull & Boar Pub sign, swinging in the breeze.

"Come on, you need a good stiff drink," Bryce says.

I nod, not wanting to leave my pity party quite yet.

"Maybe several." Reid chuckles behind me.

The first sign of a smile cracks my stone demeanor. "You still need to get your face looked at. Your laugh sounds too nasally."

He laughs again, proving my point. "Tomorrow. Tonight, I'll wear my war wounds proudly."

"War wounds?" Bryce asks, finding our usual table in the back. "You look like a mass casualty."

Reid touches his nose with a wince, doing his best to hide the pain.

"I deserved it."

"Yeah, you did," I mutter quietly. The crowd is unusually thick, not a typical Sunday night. What on earth is drawing everyone here? Perhaps it's the full moon bringing everyone out.

We order a round of drinks from a passing waitress and then another not five minutes later. Being here reminds me of Gia and how we tried to hide our relationship so the public wouldn't find out. A lot of good that did. The press got more than their fair share last night. And from what I read, only part of it was true.

After the fourth round, my mood finally starts to lift. I slam the empty mug down, drawing Reid and Bryce's attention.

"We need a plan."

Bryce claps his hands, rubbing them together. "Yes, what were you thinking?"

I spin the empty glass in my hands. "Not sure. I hadn't gotten that far yet."

"I've got it." Reid empties his mug and wipes his mouth on the back of his hand. "Tomorrow, you book the earliest flight out of here to Chicago and show up at her door, flowers in hand, professing your love and devotion to her."

I raise a brow. "That sounds like it's straight out of a cheesy romantic comedy."

"Yeah, but women love those," Bryce says with a laugh.

"True. I wasn't opposed to groveling on my knees for forgiveness."

"That works too." Reid smirks, but it freezes on his face as he peers at something over my shoulder.

"What are you looking at?"

He shakes his head. "Nothing. I thought I saw something."

I tilt my head to the side, bringing my ear closer to the conversation of the table next to ours. I try not to eavesdrop, but their conversation is so loud, it's hard not to overhear.

"Did you see the new bartender? She's so hot."

"And a foreigner. Wherever Matt found her, I need to go there."

New bartender? Matt hasn't hired anyone in months, probably years. And a female, no less.

"Did you get her number?"

"No, she said she already has a boyfriend. All I know is he's one lucky bastard."

Bryce and Reid share a knowing glance. "Hey Luke, since it's taking the waitress so long, why don't you head to the bar and get the next round."

"You assholes are so lazy." Grabbing the empty mugs, I weave my way through the crowd, finding the only open spot at the bar. Those guys weren't kidding. Matt really did hire a new female bartender. Her skinny jeans hug her ass like a second skin while her long brown hair flows in waves down her back.

My heart kicks up a notch and I practically drop the glasses on the floor.

I know that ass, felt it beneath my palms without any barriers between us.

There's no way fate has blessed us twice.

When she turns to smile at the retreating customer, the world shifts and practically stops turning.

My angel.

Our eyes lock as she walks my way, the smile never once faltering on her beautiful face.

For a minute, I forget how to breathe. The black fitted shirt shows off her delicate curves.

She's the most beautiful creature I've ever seen in my life.

It was true when I first saw her in Chicago and it's still true to this day.

"Hey handsome. What can I get you?"

CHAPTER
Six

Luke

She's here, not on some flight heading halfway around the world away from me. Instead, standing before me like a vision, one so sweet and pure I want to pinch myself to make sure I'm not dreaming.

I focus on her moving lips—those plump, juicy lips I want to bite into—but I can't hear a word she says over the thrumming of blood rushing through my ears.

"Luke?" Her voice finally breaks through, though it sounds like we're in a tunnel. "Luke? Are you okay?"

"You're here," I say on an exhale. I hadn't noticed when I started holding my breath.

Gia cracks a small smile. "I am."

The demanding organ in my chest practically commands release with each erratic beat against my ribcage. "I-I was afraid you'd flown back to Chicago."

Slowly, she shakes her head. "I thought about it, but decided against it."

"I'm glad." For the first time in hours, a full-fledged smile graces my lips. "And you're working here?"

She laughs, the sound delighting my ears. "Yeah, Matt was kind enough to give me a job since I plan on staying for a while."

Hope blossoms in my chest at her words. "Good. Good." Why do I suddenly feel so nervous? This woman is my world, whether she knows it or not. Even though she was unsure of our relationship over the last few weeks, now more than ever, I will show her what I have planned for us.

A group of unruly guys walk through the door, drawing her attention slightly. They eye her up with drunken smiles, sending the hair on the back of my neck to stand on end.

Gia places a hand on my arm, calming me down. "Relax. If I'm going to work here, you'll have to get used to the ogling."

Matt smirks behind her. "She's right. Comes with the job."

"Doesn't mean I have to like it," I say, giving her hand a squeeze before releasing her. The group bellies up to the bar, hooting and hollering for attention. Before she turns away, I grab her elbow, holding her back. "Can we talk later?"

She smiles and nods. "I'm working until close, but we can talk after."

"I can wait a few hours. I'll be at our usual table."

With a wink, she leaves me to help her new customers. Thank God we still have a chance.

Reid and Bryce sport similar grins as I retake my seat. Traitors.

"You couldn't warn me?"

Bryce shakes his head. "Hey, we were just as shocked. It's not our fault you always sit with your back to the bar."

"Assholes." They chuckle, pulling my own smile. "You're still on my shit list," I say, pointing to Reid.

He holds his hands up in defense. "At least we found her and she's here."

Very true.

Bryce looks to the table with his brows drawn. "Um, did you get the drinks?"

Shit.

I flag down the waitress and order two rounds immediately, knowing an immense amount of alcohol will be needed if I have to endure Gia flirting for tips while sitting in the back watching.

Reid and Bryce stay with me until Matt yells for bar close. I told them it wasn't necessary, but they refused to listen.

We stay in our seats, watching Matt and Gia go through the closing procedures. It's amazing how quickly she picks things up. You'd never know it was her first shift tonight with how expertly she handled things behind the bar. Remembering everyone's drink choice, tending to those patiently waiting, filling the waitress's orders. Not once looking overwhelmed or confused. In fact, the smile she's still sporting has been plastered on her face most of the night.

It's a smile I could look at every day and never be tired of it.

The three of us grab some rags and start wiping down tables and turning up chairs. We don't want to be a burden for staying after close and not help. My intentions are more selfish. The faster she cleans up, the faster we can talk.

Matt nods and thanks us for the assistance. "I'd hire you to help close, but I don't think it'd go over well with Her Majesty."

I roll my eyes. "Nothing ever does."

He looks between me and Gia and nods. "See you tomorrow night?"

She gives him a mock salute. "You know where to find me."

Handing her an envelope, he wishes the rest of us good night and disappears through the back entrance.

Bryce walks up to Gia and shoves her shoulder.

"Ow! What the fuck?"

Before she can protest more, he engulfs her in a bone-crushing hug, leaving her little choice but to return the gesture.

"Don't you *ever* fucking scare me like that again."

She laughs and pats his back, trying to tap out. "I'm sorry."

"Not yet but you will be." He pulls back, his eyes rimmed slightly red. "Come on, let's go home."

That delectable bottom lip disappears between her teeth. "Um, I kind of am home."

What?

Gia kicks an invisible rock and looks down. "I, uh, live upstairs."

"No, you have a place," Bryce says. "We've talked about this."

"You know I can't stay there when your sister is still pissed at me. Not to mention seeing the judgment on your parents' faces. I don't think I can take it. At least not yet. Besides, the birds need to leave the nest at some point. I have a great little place that's clean and close to work. What more can a girl ask for?"

I have several ideas, but none are appropriate to vocalize in present company.

Knowing he's not winning this battle, Bryce gives her another hug. "We'll discuss this again soon."

Gia laughs and kisses his cheek. "Whatever helps you sleep at night."

She starts shutting down the lights, keeping Reid hidden in the shadows. Just to make sure, he pulls the hat lower on his brow. You can practically feel the shame and regret pouring off his body.

With a yawn, Gia stretches her arms above her head. "Look, guys, I'm sorry I scared you, but it's been a long day and I'm in desperate need of sleep. I promise I'll be here tomorrow."

Satisfied with her answer, Bryce and Reid follow behind out the back door and round the building to the car. Bryce stops at the sidewalk, looking over his shoulder.

"Luke, you coming?"

I'm not leaving here without talking to Gia. Whether it's tonight or tomorrow, I don't care. But we will be having this conversation. "Go on without me. If I need a ride, I'll call David."

"No, it's okay. We can talk later," she says, taking a step back.

Unacceptable. "I'm not leaving until we talk."

Wrapping her arms around her waist, she looks off to the side. "Like I said, I'm really tired and I don't know if I have the energy for this conversation."

Bryce and Reid look to each other, unsure of what to do. I wave them off, letting them know I'll be okay, leaving the two of us standing alone in the quiet night.

"Ugh, you're a stubborn man," she says, turning her back and stomping up the wooden stairs leading to the third story of the building.

She was right about the place. It's clean and tidy. Small compared to what she left behind, but that never suited her. Gia's not the kind of girl who needs all the frills and best of everything. Give her a hot dog and a beer and she's content.

The door quietly clicks behind us as I walk further into the space, noting the minimal furniture and extremely tiny kitchen area.

"It reminds me of your place back in Chicago," I say, turning around to meet her eyes.

She flashes a proud smile and sits on the couch. "Right? A

bit smaller but livable." I raise a brow which causes her to laugh. "Okay, a lot smaller. But it's a great location, close to shops and restaurants since I don't have a car, and work is literally at my doorstep."

I join her on the couch, keeping a little space between us. It's taking all my strength to not rip her clothes off and bury myself inside her. This conversation is important. We need to work through the events from last night, or hell, the last week.

Gia fidgets with her fingers in her lap, keeping her focus on everything but me. No. That won't do.

Lifting her chin, I give her a warm smile, hopefully letting her know that everything will be okay, that we will make it through this.

"About last night," I start, swallowing hard. I've spoken to many foreign heads and dignitaries over the years. Public speaking is part of my duty, yet my tongue is tied in a knot staring at the angel before me.

Pink tinges her cheeks as she tries to look away again. "How did everything get so messed up? I was trying to give you time like you wanted, and then the next minute I see you in the arms of another woman. Do you know how that felt?"

"As a matter of fact, I do. Like watching someone else's lips on the one you want the most."

She pales slightly, her bottom lip quivering on a deep breath. "I didn't want it." Her voice is barely above a whisper. "You have to believe me."

Fuck it. I slide closer until our knees touch and I cradle her cheek in my palm, wiping away a stray tear with my thumb. "Angel, of course I believe you. It took a minute for my brain to catch up."

"But why?" She jerks her head back, letting my hand fall to

my lap. "You know me, Luke. You know my feelings for you are real. How could you ever think I would betray you with your best friend? Do you know how much that hurt? You know your mother is plotting against us, yet you believed her words without question or pause. I'm here for you. Only you. I deserved for you to give me the benefit of the doubt."

"I know, and I will apologize until the word loses its meaning. Hindsight is always twenty-twenty. Looking back on the scenario, I saw the shock and hurt on your face as it happened, listened to the poison my mother was slinging and fell right into her trap. She preyed on my vulnerability and fears and I'm ashamed that I allowed it to happen. I can't even begin to explain how furious I am at her backhanded tactics. I don't know the reasons yet for this interference, but I will find out."

"How am I supposed to trust you when you didn't have faith in us?"

The pain on her face cracks my heart in two. This mess is my fault. I would do anything to erase the events of the last twenty-four hours.

The door bursts open, swinging both our gazes to the sudden intrusion. Instinctively, I move in front of Gia, needing to protect her from the potential invader. Reid stands in the doorway, shoulders set back and chest slightly heaving. Did he run all the way here from his house?

Gia moves from behind me, knowing there isn't any danger. "Reid, what in the hell are you doing?"

His eyes bounce between the two of us, unsure where to look first. "I have to talk to you."

I ball my fists tightly at my sides, trying to keep the jealous monster at bay. Was his apology this morning a lie? Did he only help me find her in order to keep her for himself?

Reid takes notice of my offensive stance, instantly putting his hands up. "I swear, I'm not here to cause trouble."

"That depends on what comes out of your mouth," I grit out.

He steps out of the shadows, causing Gia to gasp. "What in the hell happened to your face?" She rushes over and gently brushes a fingertip across his nose and under his eyes, the skin more purple than it was a few hours ago.

Our eyes lock briefly before Reid looks away. "Karma."

Gia swings her gaze to me. "Seriously? You beat him up?"

"We were working it out," I say, shrugging my shoulders.

"Men," she mutters under her breath as she drags Reid to the chair opposite the couch. "I don't have anything frozen to put on your swollen face, but I can run downstairs to the bar and grab some ice. Why didn't you go to the hospital to get this checked out?"

He sheepishly looks between us. "We were busy this afternoon."

This time Gia looks down and away. "I'm sorry."

"No, you have nothing to be sorry for," he says, reaching for her hand, but thinking better of it he retracts it right away. "I'm the selfish asshole who put a wedge between you two. Anyone with eyes could see how much you care for each other and I let jealousy drive me mad. I wanted you both to know that I'm going to help any way I can with whatever you need."

"Reid, you've already apologized this morning at your house. There's no need to apologize again." Gia reclaims her seat on the couch, but I choose to keep standing. I still don't fully trust Reid yet.

"There is. I hurt two people I care deeply for. I know my actions come with consequences and if losing your friendship is it, then I'll be profoundly sorry for the rest of my life. But, if there's a way I can help mend what I've torn, I will do anything."

Am I willing to throw away a lifelong friendship over this? His sincerity is evident, as well as his need for atonement.

"I still need a bit of time to forgive you," Gia says. "But you know I will. You're my friend. It was a mistake and you're willing to make it right. I can appreciate that."

He tries to smile but winces instead. Shit, I really hope I didn't break his face too much.

Gia shoots me a chilling glance before huffing a sigh. "I'll be back. Stay right there and no fighting. Both of you." She waves a finger between us and quickly runs out the door.

Uncomfortable silence fills the space. There's never been this awkwardness between Reid and me before. Then again, he's never tried to steal my girl.

"Listen, Gia mentioned something this morning that was weird and I didn't think of it until we left you two," he says, sitting with his arms resting between his knees. "She asked me if you and Kiera were betrothed. Wonder where she would have gotten an idea like that?"

"Betrothed? What is this, the sixteenth century?" The lightbulb clicks on, causing my jaw to lock again. I can't believe how ruthless my mother is. Not only was she feeding on my fears, but Gia's as well. Now Kiera's sudden interest makes sense. Mother probably encouraged her to pursue me, saying it was practically a done deal.

"Yeah, I thought the same thing. Poor Gia looked offended when I laughed in her face. Your mother is definitely up to something."

"Yes, and not caring who she uses in the process. Kiera is an innocent party in all this. The fact she's using her as a pawn is disgusting."

Reid nods. "So what are we going to do? Someone should warn Kiera."

"No, we need her." An idea pops into my head, one filled with revenge. "I'll talk to her and see if I can get her to switch sides. She and I can stage a few photo ops, letting my mother think her plan has worked and then expose her for the venomous snake she is."

His eyes widen. "You think that's a good idea? Kiera will still get hurt. Isn't there another way?"

I swallow hard. "I don't know. Possibly." Nick's brief conversation from last night pops into my head. Why was he so cryptic? Something's going on there. Something big. "Either way, I'll protect everyone who needs it."

"I hope you're right. Trying to take your mother down will be harder than you think."

"Probably, but no one needs to know how deceitful their queen is. We just need to let her know we won't play by her rules. I'm not about to take down the crown. Just her."

"If you say so."

The door creaks open again. Gia holds a plastic bag filled with ice and a clean bar rag. Kneeling down beside the chair, she makes a cold press for Reid and hands it to him. "Put this on your face right now, or so help me I'll call an ambulance to take you in."

He cracks a slight smile and follows orders, flinching at the cold assault. Gia sits back on her heels, keeping careful watch. "Glad to see you two didn't kill each other while I was gone."

I stand behind her and massage her shoulders, feeling the muscles let go with each pass of my fingers. "I told you, we worked it out this morning."

"By using him as a punching bag? Reid, did you even defend yourself?"

His one uncovered eye jerks to the left. "Maybe?"

She sighs. "So that's a no. Look, I refuse to get between two friends. I don't do triangles. I can barely handle straight lines. If there's going to be an issue, tell me now and I'll go back to Chicago and things can get back to normal."

"No," we both shout at the same time.

"No issue," Reid says, taking her hand. "I promise. There won't be any more trouble from me for you two."

He hands her the compress, but she pushes it back to his face. "Take it with you. I will be calling in the morning to make sure you've seen the doctor."

"I promise." Keeping the rag over his nose and one eye, he makes his way to the door and turns before walking through. "You two have a good night." With a parting smirk, he walks away, leaving the two of us in the middle of her living room floor.

I keep my hands on her shoulders, needing to touch her, simply to reassure myself she's still here and not gone. Thinking about the possibility sends an ache through my heart again. "Gia," I say, lifting her off the floor and pressing her back against my chest. "I'm truly, madly, deeply sorry for my actions."

She leans her head against my shoulder. "You can't use a 90s love ballad to get into my good graces again."

I chuckle and spin her around, running my hand up her neck, feeling the pulse quicken with every slide of my touch. "But it can't hurt, right?"

Her tiny fist connects with my shoulder. "You can't joke your way out of this either." She wiggles out of my hold and takes her place on the couch again. "Do you know how much you hurt me? It's not the fact you needed a moment to get your head on straight. It's the fact you thought the actions were even plausible. Not once in all the time we've known each other have I made any declarations to Reid or acted even remotely close to how I act with you. Yet your mother says something and instantly I'm the American whore trying to worm her way into the crown."

I close the distance between us and drop to my knees before her. "You are *nothing* like my mother says. Those words are never to cross your mind or lips again." Placing my hands on her knees, I run them slowly up her thighs until they find their home on her waist. "I won't make excuses for my actions because there aren't any. You're right. I knew my mother was trying to put a wedge between us and allowed her to prey on my fears rather than putting trust in our relationship. But I swear to you now, on God and country, that will *never* happen again." To further my point, I rest my head in her lap and hold on tight. Groveling on my knees was always an option. "I'm throwing myself at your mercy. My heart is in your hands, Gia Hartley. I only pray you never let it go."

CHAPTER
Seven

Gia

How can I stay mad after a speech like that? Not that I was truly mad. Irritated, yes. Especially after seeing what he did to poor Reid. The fact he beat the shit out of him earlier and then the two of them act like nothing happened baffles me. But I'm not about to deconstruct the male brain at the moment.

I run my fingers through his dark, thick hair, closing my eyes briefly. I've always had a love affair with these silky strands. Normally, we'd be in the throes of passion and ecstasy, gripping them tight or holding on for dear life as he ravages my body and soul. This tender moment is almost as sweet.

"Luke, get up. You're going to ruin your knees," I say, moving my ministrations to his shoulders and neck, hoping to coax him into a more comfortable position.

He shakes his head, turning his nose directly between my legs. Instinct takes over as I massage his scalp and slide my hips ever so slightly down the cushion. I can feel his smile against my jean-clad thighs, twisting his head again to elicit a soft moan, laced with desire.

How does he know how to make me weak with little to no effort? Everything south of my navel contracts as he digs deeper between my legs, pushing them open with his hands to gain better access.

"Let me show you how sorry I am," he says gruffly. Not going to lie, the rough edge to his voice is turning me on more than his wandering fingers up the inside of my thighs.

With deft dexterity, he tugs the zipper down on my jeans, teasing my skin as he slides them off and tosses them over his shoulder. He regains his position, gripping my hips to set me on the edge of the cushion, practically open for his viewing pleasure. The only thing stopping him is the thin barrier of my thong, which might as well be nonexistent.

Luke runs his nose up my seam. "Christ, Gia, you smell so sweet." He pulls the fabric to the side, giving him full access to my aching core. Once his tongue connects with my clit, it's game over. I perch my heels on the edge of the couch, opening myself more for his devilish ways. "Like nectar of the gods."

Letting my head fall back against the cushion, I grip his hair tight, keeping him anchored to my body, wanting everything he has to give. My moans start soft but grow louder with each lap of his tongue, practically screaming his name as he inserts two fingers inside me, putting pressure exactly where I need it.

"Fuck... Luke..." Thank God I don't have a downstairs neighbor. If we ever decide to have a little afternoon delight, I'll need to make sure Matt isn't using the office on the second floor, otherwise he's going to get quite the earful.

I pick my head up when he stops. "You weren't fond of these

panties, were you?" He takes the fabric in two hands, ripping them easily before I could answer. Even if I was, it didn't matter.

"I'll buy new ones."

"The fuck you will," he growls. "As long as I'm here, panties are optional. One more thing to get in the way."

Not wasting time, he sucks and licks his way up my center, teasing me with slow and fast movements, turning my brain into mush as I try to focus on anything and everything he's doing. It's pointless. The way he expertly plays my body leaves me helpless to his touch, bringing me to the peak before backing off, leaving me dangling off the edge. There's no end to his sweet torture. My body is wound so tight I'm afraid it'll snap at any minute if I don't find release.

"Please, Luke, please," I pant out, barely able to breathe.

He takes pity and twists his fingers inside me while sucking on my clit, throwing me over the edge into a never-ending abyss of pleasure.

Sounds and lights disappear as the orgasm rips through my body. Luke eagerly laps at my pulsing pussy, cleaning up every last drop.

I rest a hand on my forehead, desperately clinging to any semblance of sanity I have left, though I'm sure it's been scattered across the apartment floor.

Luke kisses his way up my stomach, taking the shirt with him until he tosses it to the floor, joining my abandoned jeans. "I'm sorry," he says, sweeping his lips across mine, letting me taste my tangy essence.

I nod and kiss him back. "We should fight more often."

He chuckles and takes a seat on the couch, pulling me onto his lap. "Angel, we don't need to fight to have amazing sex."

"Yeah, but make-up sex is *way* hotter than regular sex."

One brow raises to his hairline, clearly amused. "Is that a challenge?"

I pull the sweater over his head and shoulders, evening the playing field. "If you want to take it as such, be my guest." His muscles tighten and release as I explore the vast expanse of exposed skin before me. Damn, his body is a work of art. I know how busy his schedule is. The fact he still has time to take care of himself is nothing short of amazing. I wish I had his discipline.

But they say you burn as many calories during sex as you would running five miles.

I want to run twenty miles tonight.

Whatever fatigue I had earlier is gone. The beast is awake and hungry.

Lifting myself slightly off his lap, I make quick work of his jeans and boxers. Luke helps me along—well, lifts his hips while sliding a finger inside me as a distraction. I take him in my hand, rubbing his cock along my slick entrance, teasing him to return the favor. He groans and throws his head back while gripping my hips.

"Fuck, Gia. You best hurry or I won't last long."

Well, that won't do.

Without another thought, I plunge down and take his whole length in one movement.

Glorious.

There's nothing better than being filled by Luke, in any way.

I rock my hips gently, creating a small amount of friction to ignite the fire again. He doesn't make a move other than to unclasp my bra, setting my breasts free to his tongue and fingers.

"Gia, angel, you feel too good." His eyes open, widening a little. "Fuck, the condom is in my pants pocket."

I shift my hips again, letting him slide deeper inside me. The skin-on-skin contact isn't something I want to give up right now. For once, I want to feel all of him without a barrier. Even if it's for a little while.

"Not yet," I pant out, pulling out all the moves as I ride him hard, practically shaking the couch with our movements.

He grabs my hips and turns me around, propping my feet on the edge of the couch to enter me from behind. My thighs burn as I hold the position, letting him pound into my aching pussy, hitting depths I never thought were reachable. I loll my head back, finally able to move and take him at my own pace. The flames lick higher inside me, threatening to burn me to ashes in a matter of minutes.

The rational part of me knows I need to grab that condom. But each stroke of his cock makes the task seem daunting. Do we really need it?

We roll over again, putting my face into the cushions as Luke changes positions, grabbing my hips until they practically bruise while continuing his assault.

"Fuck, Gia, I'm... I'm..."

Before he has the chance to finish, my walls clench around him, releasing all the tension at once as I come hard, bringing him over the edge with me. His cock pulses inside me, releasing every drop of cum until it's practically dripping out the side.

My name is a litany on his lips, praising me with his mouth as he trails it up my spine, refusing to remove our connection.

"Okay, I concede. We don't need to fight to have amazing sex."

Luke laughs and pulls me down on top of him, still buried to the hilt. "You should know I'm always right."

"Hmm, we'll see." I turn my head and kiss him hard. Our tongues twirl together, dragging the remaining air from my lungs.

He hardens inside me and I pull back, raising a brow. "Again?"

Moving some sweat-slicked hair from my forehead, he kisses my lips before dragging my bottom one through his teeth. "I told you I wanted to apologize."

Who am I to tell him no?

CHAPTER
Eight

Gia

H oly. Fucking. Shit.

I can't remember a time where I've had this much sex. No, I take it back. The last time was with Luke in my apartment. At least then we got a few hours of sleep between sessions. Ever since our talk, it's been nonstop, pausing only a couple of times for some water.

The entire apartment smells like sex. From the living room to the kitchen to the bathroom, now my bedroom as we lay naked trying to catch our breath on the full-size bed.

"At some point, we will need to sleep," I say, swallowing hard, feeling my lungs inflate with each drag of air.

Luke only chuckles and kisses my shoulder. "We can sleep when we're dead."

"Which might be soon if we keep this up. Is there such a thing as death by sex?"

"Would you like to find out?"

I force myself to roll to my side, propping a hand under my head. "Not really. I want to live a long time and have old people sex with you."

"I like the sound of that," he says, kissing the back of my hand.

The marathon we ran has drained every ounce of energy from my body. I know he doesn't need a magic blue pill to help him out in that department, but good Lord, did he ingest a bunch of ginseng and not tell me? I'm going to be bowlegged all day if we keep this up.

An alarm buzzes somewhere in the apartment. With everything strung from one place to the other, who knows what it could be.

Luke slowly stands and searches for his phone. I roll onto my back and close my eyes until he walks back into the room.

Click. Click. Click. Click.

"Who are you texting so early in the morning? Wait, what time is it?" There's barely sunlight peeking through the tiny window in the room.

He smirks and places the phone on the nightstand. "My assistant to cancel my day. I don't plan on leaving your sight."

I sit up and drag him down onto the bed next to me. "I appreciate the gesture, but this will *not* win me points with your mother."

Pulling me down the mattress, Luke crawls over my body, hovering without touching to force our eyes to lock. "I don't give a shit what my mother thinks. After the stunt she pulled, she's lucky I even want to keep the crown."

"Don't say things like that." I shove him to the side and pull the covers over us. "I will not be the woman who destroys the royal family and traditions that date back centuries."

"It's my choice," he says, lacing our fingers together.

"I get a say in this too. We need to start communicating otherwise this won't work."

He nods, understanding my concerns. "From now on, I'll discuss everything with you."

I smile and brush my lips against his. "Thank you." Now onto a more important matter. "Speaking of discussions, we need to talk about the last few hours."

Luke quirks a brow. "What about them? Still not satisfied?"

My cheeks heat instantly. "Hardly. No, I'm more concerned about the lack of condoms. I know I said the first time I'd grab it and then it was too good to bother once we started. But we failed to put them on after that. Are you… I mean, is this…" God, how can I not form the words?

"Gia, I'm clean." He grazes the backs of his fingers across my flaming cheeks, trailing them down the column of my throat before placing his hand above my heart. "I make it a point to check myself every six months. Not because I sleep around with lots of women, but because it's part of the health directive put forth by my mother."

Oh, thank God. Not that I expected him to be celibate but knowing he doesn't sleep around somehow makes me feel better. "Same. Not the checking every six months, but I don't sleep around either."

His grin stretches from ear to ear. "Good. Now I don't have to stuff my pockets every time I want to come see you." The smile slips slightly. "Are you…?"

Oh, the other thing. "Yes, I have an IUD in, so we're covered from any accidents."

I close my eyes as he runs his hand over my cheek, threading his fingers in my hair as he pulls my face to his. "Nothing we ever do or make would be an accident. Remember that."

We're not ready for this conversation yet, especially coming off our first misunderstanding. Not to mention it's too early to be discussing babies.

A loud yawn escapes my lips, effectively breaking the mood. "Sorry. It's been a long couple of days."

Luke sheepishly looks down and pulls me into his chest. "And I'm partly to blame. Allow me to make amends right now." We kiss slowly, deeply, lazily until every muscle in my body relaxes in his arms. "There. That's better. Let's get some sleep, angel. We have all the time in the world today."

"Technically the day ends at midnight, so it's a set number of hours."

My cheek bounces against his chest as he chuckles. "I love your smart mouth."

Without another word, we fall into the most restful sleep I've had in a long, long time.

The calling of nature brings me from my slumber as I stretch my arms above my head, reminding me how sore my muscles are after the intense workout. I've never met a man with so much stamina before. Then again, most of the guys I met before barely made it to a second date. And the handful that did were no comparison. As much as my bladder would appreciate the relief, I can't pull myself away from Luke. He looks so peaceful lying there, lashes fanned across his cheeks. Even a hint of a smile gracing his lips.

I know we've barely established what we are, but after everything that's happened, I know we're more than what the world knows and sees. There's only so long I'm able to deny my true feelings.

But I'm not ready to give them a voice. Not yet. It's not that I'm worried he doesn't feel the same way. I can tell in his actions and face how much I mean to him. No, it's the obstacles before us creating my hesitation.

I know he was joking earlier about giving up the crown, but it wasn't funny. He loves his country and I won't be the one who tears everything apart.

We'll find a way to make this work.

"I can hear you thinking. Go back to sleep," he lazily groans, using his damned bedroom voice.

I kiss the tip of his nose and wiggle out of his arms. "In a minute. There's something I need to do first."

He pops his eyes open and runs his hand up my spine as I sit on the edge of the bed. "Need any company?"

"For this? No. Maybe when I shower." Hopefully the look I'm giving over my shoulder is enticing and sexy. It must have worked because his eyes light up at the prospect.

"Say the word and I'll make sure you get clean."

I laugh. "I've heard those words before. And they were lies."

Before he has the chance to rebut my statement, I make a beeline for the bathroom, using the time to freshen up a bit before climbing back into bed.

Back in the safety of his arms, I nuzzle his chest, letting the few hairs tickle my nose. "I missed you."

I shake my head. "I was barely gone five minutes."

His lips find the curve of my neck, nipping and sucking a path up to my ear and down to my shoulder, leaving my skin erupting in goose bumps. "Any time away from you is too long."

Words and thoughts leave my head as he continues his ministrations. How am I supposed to string a coherent sentence together?

"Luke, as much as I want to stay here in this bed with you,

we need to get up and do something or my stomach will eat itself." To further my point, the organ growls with the strength of a grizzly bear, causing Luke to pull back and chuckle.

"We can't have that." He kisses me once more. "I'm at your disposal today, madam. Whatever you want, consider it yours."

Oh, that sounds dangerous. And so many possibilities. "Really? My, my, my, where do I begin?"

His pupils dilate as he rolls on top of me. "I can think of a few things."

I entertain his idea for half a second before rolling us over again, retaking the power. "As much as I want to stay here all day, I do have to work tonight, which means we don't have a lot of free time. And Matt may get a little upset if I'm late, especially considering I'm two floors up."

He playfully frowns. "Ugh, fine. First, we need to shower… *my way.*"

Won't argue with that idea.

His shower tactic put us a half hour behind, forcing us to stay within walking distance of my apartment. Which really was the plan anyway. If I'm going to be here for a while, I'll need to know the neighborhood.

Walking hand in hand, we pass several stores and shops that pique my interest. Luke entertains my window-shopping obsession and promised he won't buy anything I mentioned. Not that I believe him. I wouldn't be surprised to see a package or two dropped off at my back steps.

A few blocks over, we find a cute little café with the most divine smells coming from inside. My stomach voices its displeasure at still being empty.

"You weren't kidding when you said your stomach is eating itself."

I squeeze his hand and drag him inside. "Don't mess with a girl and her food."

"Noted."

The host seats us immediately, putting us in a rounded booth secluded in the back, mostly away from the prying eyes of the public. There's nothing like being alone out in the open. Except for the stares and whispers of the patrons we walk past. Now I know how a fish feels trying to swim around in its bowl.

Something catches Luke's eye, causing him to straighten his back and harden his expression.

Odd.

"Hey, are you okay?" Finally, he looks at me, but something is off. His smile is forced, not like it was outside before we got here.

"Of course. Just hungry is all."

Maybe it's the fact we're in a very public place shortly after the destructive headlines and photos, tarnishing his name and possibly his reputation. Guilt takes over as I quietly look over the menu, suddenly not feeling quite as hungry as I was five minutes ago.

"This place is excellent. They make their pasta from scratch."

Even though my appetite has dropped, my stomach hasn't received the message. Everything sounds amazing. Florentine tortellini with shrimp, steak with béarnaise sauce, garlic pork tenderloin with a pomegranate chutney.

"How do you choose? I could literally order everything on the right side of the menu and still want more," I say, trying to inject some of the levity back between us.

For a moment, it works. He pushes his glasses up his nose and laughs. "I believe it. It's rare to see a woman with a healthy appetite. Most of the women in court eat so daintily, like breathing would make them gain five pounds."

"After all the sex we had last night—or early this morning I guess—I need to replace a bunch of calories."

I need to remind him of the connection between us. For whatever reason, something doesn't feel right. Like there's an ominous omen lurking in the shadows.

His eyes bounce back and forth, tracing my features. His palm warms my cheek in a gentle caress, making my eyelids flutter of their own will.

Closing the distance between us, I press my lips against his, doing my best to keep it chaste to not draw any unwanted attention. Only it's too chaste, almost stiff, like kissing a relative goodbye at the end of the night.

A clearing of a throat pulls us away. The waiter looks between us with an amused expression. "What can I get for you two?"

I try to pick up the menu, but Luke gently pries it from my hands, giving them both to the waiter. "We'll each have the Tuscan chicken pasta with Caesar salads."

He really does know me. And there is nothing sexier than a man knowing exactly what you want. It means he pays attention, listens to your likes and dislikes, and genuinely cares for your feelings.

Maybe I'm still tired, which could explain why I feel so out of sorts and am imagining things that aren't really there.

"I'll be right back." Luke stands abruptly, disappearing down a small hallway. Not a minute later, the man across the restaurant he's been staring at follows him. He probably needs to use the bathroom. Nothing suspicious, yet I can't help thinking something is off. Within seconds, my phone lights up with a notification.

Luke: Trust me.

What does he mean, trust him? And why is he messaging me in the bathroom?

When he returns to the table, he reaches for my hand and rubs his thumb along the back, doing very little to assuage any lingering doubts.

I want to ask him what's wrong, but I also don't want to make a scene in front of so many witnesses. I've had enough public humiliation to last a lifetime.

The food is just as delicious as it smelled. Pasta has always been my go-to comfort food, but this was beyond my expectations. The only thing that would have made it better would be the absence of the tension radiating off Luke.

"Should we get a dessert to go?"

I try to drag his attention away from the small menu the waiter left behind, but he refuses to look up.

"Look, there's something we need to discuss."

"Which sounds like a fancy way of saying 'we need to talk.'" Nothing good ever happens after that phrase.

The food in my stomach threatens to come up as Luke puts a little more space between us. What the fuck is happening?

Pain is etched across his face as he takes my hand in his. "I think we need to stop seeing each other."

Did I lose my hearing because there's no possible way I heard him correctly. "I'm sorry, what?"

His Adam's apple bobs up and down, like something is stuck in his throat. "Last night and this morning were amazing, but maybe that's where it should end. Perfect. Unscarred. Something to think fondly of in our memories."

Think fondly of? No, this cannot be happening.

"Why are you saying this? I thought we worked things out. We had a plan."

A void fills the space where my heart should be as Luke removes his hand from mine. "Things have changed."

"When? How? I-I don't understand. An hour ago we were making plans, building a foundation for our life together." A lone tear treks down my cheek, but I refuse to brush it away.

I can see the struggle in his eyes, feel the conflict within him. Why is he doing this? And why here?

"I have a duty to the crown and I must obey. I'm sorry."

Without another look, he leaves, stopping briefly at the front to settle the bill.

He left me.

What just happened?

The tears continue to flow down my cheeks, feeling every single person stare at me. So much for having enough public humiliation. What's one more to add to the list?

I need to get out of here.

Keeping my head down, I take the long way back to my apartment. Now my new safe haven is tainted. We christened every inch, filling it with so much happiness and joy. I won't be able to look at the space and not remember how we felt.

This was a mistake. I should have left for Chicago when I had the chance. There's still time. I've only had one shift with Matt, so it's not like he's really depending on me. He was doing fine before. He'll do fine without me. I'll let him know tonight.

The old wooden stairs creek and crack under my feet, mirroring the devastation in my chest. A million tiny fractures that cannot be glued back together. Not anymore. I thought we'd finally fixed everything, that he wanted a life with me. How could I have been so wrong?

I flick the lights on and damn near fall backward down the steps as I stare at the dark figure sitting on the couch.

"Hey, it's me," Luke says, putting his hands up in surrender. "We need to talk."

All the sadness I felt quickly morphs to anger. Is he crazy coming here after publicly humiliating me? Again?

I brush past him, slamming the door behind me. "Get out."

He follows me into the bedroom, grabbing my shoulders and forcing me to face him. "No. Not until you hear me out."

CHAPTER
Nine

Luke

Why in the hell was Simon in the restaurant? There was no earthly reason for him to be there. Unless... Goddamn it.

Mother would never get her own hands dirty. That's what her lackeys are for. But this was a message, telling me she's watching my every move, needing to control every aspect of my life.

This lunch was supposed to be beautiful, romantic. Spending time with Gia to reaffirm our affection for each other after everything that's happened. Instead, she forced my hand early. The plan was not supposed to be put into motion yet. Gia didn't even know about it. I was going to explain it tonight, after work to keep my promise of no more secrets. Fuck, why didn't I tell her before we left? When Simon followed me to the bathroom, I knew what I had to do.

The look on her face, watching her heart break again and acting like it wasn't affecting me was the hardest thing I've ever had to do. But that's why I'm here in her apartment. She needs to know the truth; not believe the fraud of a show I was forced to put on.

"Please, Gia, I can explain."

The fire in her eyes almost singes me, leaving flames lapping at my skin. She always says I have this Superman persona, but judging by her glare, she's burning me with her heat-ray vision.

"Fuck your explanation. Fuck you and everything you've ever said to me." She storms out of the room, heading straight for the door. No, this won't happen.

Before she gets out the door, I brace my arm across the threshold, blocking her escape. "I told you that I'd be open and honest from now on."

Her cynical laugh doesn't even sound like her. "That's rich. You think I'll believe anything you say right now?" Gia spreads her arms wide. "We had the most beautiful night and morning, making up for the misunderstanding of the gala. Everything was fine. Or so I thought. Was I wrong?"

I shake my head, wanting desperately to touch her but knowing it won't be welcome. Not yet. "You're not wrong."

She takes a step back, looking like I've slapped her with my comment. "Then what? Help me understand." A tear slips down her cheek. "Was it just sex?" Her voice is barely a whisper, trying to block the hurt and pain from showing.

I close the distance, pulling her into my arms. She fights me every step, bracing her hands against my chest. But I overpower her, cupping the back of her head until she gives up and rests it on my shoulder.

"Listen," I say, pressing her head closer to my chest. "Do you hear my heart?"

No response; her body still tense in my arms.

Stubborn woman.

I try a new tactic. Walking her over to the couch, I guide her until she's sitting on my lap, head still firmly placed on my chest.

"What you hear is more than a muscle doing its job. More than blood rushing through my veins. Each beat has a purpose. And that purpose is you, Gia." I swallow hard, hoping and praying she's listening. "I've never had an emotional connection to someone before. You're the air in my lungs, the name on my lips. Every thought leads to you."

Finally, she picks up her head, hesitant to make eye contact. That won't do. The same electrical shock travels through my fingers as I brush them against her cheek, drawing her gaze. I wrap my hand around the back of her neck, holding her exactly how she loves. With possession and passion, leaving her feeling like she's my world.

"I don't understand," she says with a small hiccup.

Moving my free hand to mirror the other, I stare deeply into her green eyes, hating that I've dimmed their shine. Hopefully I can bring it back.

"You are my everything. Surely you must know that."

She closes her eyes briefly before opening them, this time with hope. "Tell me."

I've never been so afraid in my life that my words would not be welcome. But she needs to know.

"I love you, Gia. More than anything. I would move heaven and earth to protect you, protect what we have." My heart feels like it's trying to leave my body, beating so rapidly I may need medical attention. "Please, say something."

She doesn't say anything, only stares. If she doesn't feel the same, if I've ruined everything because of my mother's spy, I don't know what I'll do.

I want to go back to this morning, before we left the apartment. When we were in our shroud of safety. Every time we take one step forward, it seems my mother finds a way to force us two steps back.

Gia's tiny hands wrap around my wrists, pulling them away. "I have to get ready for work."

The world feels like it's closing in, reminiscent of the night before when everything spiraled out of control.

"Call Matt. Tell him you're sick. I need you to understand, explain myself. We can't leave things like this."

Slowly, she stands from the couch, putting distance between us. "We won't leave things like this, but I need to clear my head."

No, we won't end this way. I won't accept it.

She caresses my cheek, giving me a smile, the first since we were outside the restaurant. "Wait for me here? I'll try to get out as soon as possible, but I can't have you downstairs. Not tonight."

Hope dares to take shape as I pray things will be okay. I've dreamed of the day that I'd confess my love to her, thought of the different ways she'd react.

This was never a scenario.

"I will do whatever you want, angel."

I watch her head back to her room, closing the door to change. All the protocol and etiquette I've been taught my entire life has not prepared me for this. Panic is not something I succumb to easily. There's never been a problem I haven't found a solution to.

Until now.

Gia steps out in a pair of skinny jeans and a loose gray shirt while tying her hair up in a messy bun.

"You look beautiful."

Her cheeks flush slightly. If I can still get this reaction from her, there's still a chance for us.

"Hardly." She checks her watch and scrunches her nose. "I have to go."

Slowly, she bends down and kisses my forehead, her lips barely brushing my skin.

"Wait for me."

As she slips out the door, I hang my head and brace my arms on my knees, doing exactly what she wants.

Wait.

I have no idea what time it is when she finally comes back to the apartment. The space seemed so empty without her here, I was practically going insane. So, I decided to tidy up a little after our sex marathon this morning, which did not kill enough time. After a while I had David run me a sandwich and tea from the deli down the street for a break in the path I was wearing from one side of the living room to the other. Leaving a person alone with their thoughts is dangerous, almost like giving them a loaded gun. You replay every event over and over, wondering what you could have done better or different. Would it have made a difference?

Gia sets her keys on the small hook next to the door. "Hey." She looks around, avoiding my eyes. "You cleaned."

I nod. "I wanted to surprise you."

I track her movements, watching with cautious eyes as she inspects the plate I set out for her.

"For me?"

Again, I nod. "I had David pick me up a sandwich. Thought you might appreciate one after work as well."

A smile finally cracks her lips as she heartily digs into the food, sitting in the chair opposite me in her tiny living room. Her eyes practically roll into the back of her head as she moans with delight.

"You'll have to tell me where you got this. I may need to stock up on these for after my shifts."

Little does she know I already made an arrangement with the deli owner to deliver her a meal or two during the week. Her favorite sandwiches and a few salads I'm sure she'll enjoy. I stocked a few of them already in her fridge.

"Just a little place down the street I know."

Quiet fills the space again as she slowly chews, still avoiding my stare. The suspense is killing me. If she rejects me, or refuses to hear me out, I don't know what I'll do.

"Gia, I—"

"Wait," she says, holding up her hand as she finishes her food. "I have something to say first."

For a moment, my heart stops as panic takes over. The neutral tone of her voice is making it impossible to read her thoughts. Damn, it's like she went to the same school as I did. Control your emotions and facial features during business. Never get emotional for it shows weakness.

But this woman brings me to my knees effortlessly. I'd make every deal known to man if it brought her happiness.

She blows out a quick breath, closes her eyes briefly to regroup, then—finally—meets my gaze.

"Luke, it's been a rough couple of days. I'm not one to take a ride on an emotional rollercoaster that doesn't end."

My hands start to shake so I quickly clasp them together,

hanging them between my knees to hide my nervousness. To my surprise, Gia takes my hands into hers, a smile splaying across her face. Once again, hope is kindled.

"But you are worth every twist and turn in this crazy ride called life. I know your intentions were good. However, you must know how much that hurt today, being blindsided without a warning. I thought... I thought..."

"No," I say, pulling her from her seat and onto my lap. "Never. The thought of losing you kills me more than anything ever has or could."

I brush the hair away from her face, needing to see all of her. The light returns to her eyes as she smiles, finally stretching from ear to ear.

"So it's not just me."

"No, it's not only you." Relief floods through me as I run my thumbs along her cheekbones, feeling her warmth beneath my palms.

"Good." She swallows hard. "Because I love you too. I have for a while, but I didn't want to seem like I had fallen too quickly or that I was alone in my feelings."

"Never doubt my love for you," I say, kissing the tip of her nose. "There's no timeline or guide on how two people should feel for each other. Attraction is instant, but growing close, getting to know the other person is what forms the bond. And you, my dear Gia, are woven directly into the fibers of my being."

Her tiny palms caress my face before she leans up and gently runs her lips over mine. Softly. Reverently. Lovingly.

"Now that we have that cleared up, I need an explanation."

Right. She deserves one.

Gia wiggles off my lap but I don't let her get far, pulling her close to my side to rest my head against hers.

"Reid and I devised a plan against my mother." She stills in my arms. "Not to worry, we're not creating a coup or anything. Just something to teach her a lesson."

"That's dangerous."

"Only for those who don't know how to play her game." I kiss the top of her head. "In fact, we're going to turn a few of her key players against her. You remember Kiera Wagner?"

She nods. "Unfortunately."

"Don't worry about her," I say with a chuckle. "She's a good friend." Gia picks her head up, but I press her back against my chest. "And yes, I'm aware of her attachment. However, it's not entirely her fault. My mother has been working and plotting to force us together. Which is why I'm going to turn Kiera to our side."

"How?"

Nerves strike up again in my stomach. This is the part I'm afraid she won't like. "By creating a fake relationship with her."

Just as predicted, she shoots straight up and keeps me at arm's length. "Are you shitting me? A fake relationship? Why on earth would she ever go for that?"

"Because we're friends and I doubt she'll like hearing the news that she was being used as a pawn in some matrimony scheme."

She sits quietly, mulling it over. "Probably. Or she was in on it with your mother. And what if this plan backfires, and she ends up even more in love with you than before or she could go running to your mom with the information, derailing your whole operation. And then we'd be right back where we were two days ago."

Did she even take a breath? "That's quite the rant. Trust me, we thought this through. I'm certain she is not in cahoots with my mother, nor is she aware of the situation." She scoffs her dis-approval. "Angel, I promise you, this will work."

"Okay, fine. But what about today? She wasn't even in the restaurant. What happened?"

I've given up trying to hold her against me. Instead, I en-twine our fingers together so we stay in constant contact. "The moment we walked in I saw something troubling." She raises a brow. "Rather, someone; more specifically a person that works for my mother."

"A spy?"

I nod. "His name is Simon. He does all her dirty work. It's how she gains intel on things happening around the country. As soon as I saw him, I knew I didn't have time to explain anything."

"Basically, he forced your hand."

"Yes. Everyone needed to believe I brought you there to end our relationship and the element of surprise was necessary to make it authentic."

She's silent again as I wait with bated breath for her reac-tion. Was it a shitty thing to do? Absolutely. Do I regret it? Yes and no. Yes for hurting her, but no because it was a starting point to the rest of our future.

I only hope she sees it the same way.

"Okay, I get it. Don't agree with your execution, but I get it." I blow out a breath, but she holds her hands out when I reach for her. "Oh, don't think you're off the hook, mister. There needs to be some serious making up for this."

"In bed?"

She laughs and all the tension finally leaves my shoulders, allowing them to slump back to their normal position. "Do you always have such a dirty mind?"

"Only when it comes to you."

Lord, I love her blush. I'd whisper all the naughty things to keep it there.

"There's one more thing," I say, keeping my hands on hers. "In order to make this believable, our sleepovers will be a bit difficult. For obvious reasons, I won't be able to sneak around town and climb through your bedroom window."

"I'd be impressed if you did, considering I'm on the third floor of the building."

"Cheeky." I roll my eyes and continue. "It doesn't mean they have to stop. The staff at my cottage are loyal to me and not my mother. David would be able to run you over there whenever you want."

Gia chews on her plump bottom lip. "Okay, this went from sweet and romantic to late-night booty calls."

"Hardly. We'll figure out a schedule."

"Now we're penciling in sex?"

Christ, why can't I explain this right? "Not at all."

She places a finger on my lips. "Before you dig yourself an even deeper hole, let me try. Since you can't come over here whenever you please due to the spies reporting your whereabouts to a certain self-important family member, our interactions will have to be held at your place, not mine. Not every day as that would draw attention, but like normal dates, when we're able to."

"That's what I said."

God help me, I love this woman. Her defiance and snark—especially when she rolls her eyes at something I say or scrunches her nose when she thinks an idea is stupid—is what makes her stand out above everyone else.

"Sure, whatever you say. And during your 'fake relationship' with Kiera, I'm assuming it means public outings?"

"Unfortunately. We'll have to sell it. But I have a plan where

I can still see you while doing both. We can go to the Boar and Bull with the others since it's already an established hangout of ours. The spies will think I'm rubbing my new relationship in your face."

"Which they're not wrong."

I silence her objection with a kiss. "They are completely wrong because the only woman I'm in a relationship with is you."

"Convince me."

Threading my fingers into her hair, I guide her mouth back to mine, teasing and tempting until she gives in, letting our tongues dance and tangle with each other. This woman is the air I breathe, giving me a life I always wanted, rather than trying to settle on something I didn't.

I guide her to lay back on the couch, pressing every inch of my body into hers, showing how much I need her.

"Still questioning my motives?"

Heat fires in her eyes, still a little dazed from our kiss. "Not anymore. Now I'm just horny and think we need to make up again."

Far be it from me to deny this woman anything she wishes.

CHAPTER
Ten

Luke

"This will work. This *will* work," I mutter under my breath before walking through the doors of the great room where my enemy waits.

Leaving Gia in the middle of the night was one of the hardest things I've ever had to do. Sneaking down the street for David to pick me up wasn't ideal, but we couldn't risk anyone seeing my driver outside the pub when it wasn't open. It wouldn't take long for someone to figure out why I was there after hours.

Luckily, our goodbye-for-now still lingers on my lips, giving me all the strength I need as I walk into the lion's den.

"Lucien, darling, so glad you could join us." Mother stands and kisses me on both cheeks, putting on her best performance for Count Wagner and Kiera.

"Of course, it was my pleasure." I bow to both of them, who return the gesture. It's times like these I wish I was back in

Chicago. No formality, no bowing and curtsying. I could blend in with the crowd and shake hands like a normal human.

"Her Majesty was kind enough to invite us over for a little midmorning tea," Kiera says, the smile beaming on her face.

I nod, sitting on the chair next to Kiera. Mother takes notice, showing her approval with a hum. It takes everything in me not to show my annoyance, schooling my features like I was trained to do for so many years.

This is nothing more than a business transaction.

Count Wagner drones on about one of his many recent trips to Hungary, making it easy to tune him out. The story stays the same, only the venue changes. A boat ride here, horseback riding there. A surprise for his wife, topped by sealing a business deal all in a matter of days.

I don't miss Kiera glancing my way every chance she can from the corner of my eye. Deep breath. It's now or never.

"Kiera, how have things been going for you? Enjoying your new position?"

For a moment, she stares at her teacup, but places it gently on the table. "Immensely. Now that I'm the primary buyer, there's so much more flexibility in my schedule, not to mention being able to travel all over the world." Kiera has been working for Vitale since she graduated university three years ago with her business and design degrees. With the help of her name, she's able to bring exclusive fashions from all over the world to their stores around Europe.

"Doesn't that sound wonderful? Almost reminds me of someone else I know." Mother smirks before taking a sip of her tea.

"I heard you made a fantastic purchase at the Milan fashion week."

Kiera beams. "It was a stroke of luck. There was a new and upcoming designer that everyone was fawning over. Daphne Walters." I shake my head when she pauses. "Well, my assistant has a mutual friend in common with her assistant and was able to get us a sit down. I knew I had to act quickly so we could retain exclusive rights to her new set. The rest is history."

"Where is she from?" I ask, not really caring other than for the sake of appearances.

"Chicago."

Mother almost chokes on her drink, barely able to save face as she sets the offending liquid down. "Oh, dear, an American? Surely her designs couldn't be *that* good."

Kiera's brows draw together. "On the contrary. Every available retailer was foaming at the mouth to get her. I was glad to have the inside track, as were my bosses. The projected sales with this line are upward to four hundred percent."

Even my mother can't argue with that. It's good business.

"Well, congratulations, my dear. Hopefully this will be the start to a prosperous career." A mischievous gleam lights her eyes, instantly putting me on alert. "Lucien, why don't you escort Ms. Wagner to her next appointment. I believe you have a meeting in the same area."

Sneaky. And good decorum would prohibit a refusal. But this would be the perfect opportunity to put my plot into motion.

"Of course. Ms. Wagner." I extend a hand, which she eagerly takes as I help her from the chair. The feel of her hand in mine isn't right, like forcing a square into a round hole. There's no charge of energy or zing of electricity flowing between us. Only friendly familiarity. Kiera must notice as well because the normal blush crossing her cheeks is missing, instead creating a little wrinkle between her brows.

This will work.

Once we're secured in the back of the car, I instruct David to head toward the city center.

"Are you hungry?"

Kiera turns and smiles politely. "A little." She glances at her watch. "I suppose there's time."

I rap my knuckles on the divider, my signal to David to set the plan into motion. Within minutes, we pull up to a familiar restaurant, drawing a slight frown from Kiera.

"Lucien, are you sure? I-I know about the incident yesterday." My brows draw together, trying to play dumb. She takes a step closer, placing a hand on my forearm. "Your mother filled me in on your breakup."

"Oh, that." I force a smile and extend an elbow to her. "We can talk about it inside."

A few people stare and whisper as we make our way to the back of the café. Kiera doesn't seem affected by the attention, which is good. Since she also grew up in the spotlight, she's learned to ignore the surroundings and focus on what's in front of her.

Within minutes, I spot a familiar face walking through the door. As predicted, Simon is here to bring back all the details of my afternoon.

Playing right into my hand.

Kiera picks up a menu, chewing on her bottom lip while mulling over the options. I stare at her intently, putting on a show for all to see. She glances up with a wayward smile.

"What? Do I have something on my face?"

I shake my head. "Not at all." A sudden bout of nerves rolls through my stomach. "Kiera, there's something I want to discuss with you."

She places the menu down and folds her hands neatly on top. "You know I'm here for whatever you need."

"Good. I'm glad to hear that. Now, without drawing too much attention, do you see the gentleman sitting by himself near the window?" She discretely pretends to grab something out of her purse, picking her head up slightly in Simon's direction.

"Yes. What about him?"

I lean in close, placing my hand on hers. "His name is Simon. He works for my mother as an intelligence gatherer."

"A spy?"

"Yes. There's something you must know. You're being played like a pawn in a chess game."

"I'm sorry, I don't understand. By whom?"

I force a smile, pretending that we're having an intimate conversation. "My mother." Before she has time to gasp, I squeeze her hand. "Don't make any surprised movements. Just smile and nod like you're agreeing to something." She complies, though fear starts setting in her eyes.

"How do you know?"

"Everything you've read in the papers regarding Gia and I was orchestrated and put forth by her. She's trying to sabotage my relationship due to some unknown dislike."

"So Gia kissing Reid was all a setup?"

I look down briefly. "No, unfortunately, that was real, but there were circumstances surrounding it that's too detailed to get into right this moment. However, she used the situation to her advantage, making sure the photographers plastered the picture all over to tarnish her name."

Kiera squeezes my hand. "And her urging me at the gala to be by your side?"

"A ploy, I'm afraid. It appears both our parents have been

pushing us together for years, even though there's nothing between us."

Something in her eyes breaks, making me feel bad for saying the truth she may have been unwilling to admit until now. A relationship between us was never going to work out. We were lifelong friends, nothing more.

"I-I know. I'm sure you knew a part of me had a secret crush on you, but I didn't want to jeopardize what we had."

"Yes, I knew. And we deserved more than settling for something our parents tried to push on us."

The waiter arrives and takes our order, giving us a quick reprieve. "So what exactly did you want to discuss?"

Taking a deep breath, I blow it out slowly, praying she understands. "I want us to fake date."

Silence. No, worse than silence. She's damn near comatose, staring at me, unblinking.

"I, you want, what?"

I scoot my chair closer and lean toward her, keeping my voice low. "I want us to fake a relationship to get even with my mother for using you and trying to run and ruin my life. What she did to you is unacceptable."

"And you. Coordinating all those scandals."

I nod. "Exactly. But I need to keep this as quiet as possible. I don't want a public outcry, more of a personal scolding. No one needs to know how wicked their beloved queen actually is. But I understand if you don't want to go through with it, given what you confessed to me just now. The last thing I want to do is hurt you." And I don't. Even though there's nothing between us, Kiera doesn't deserve to get hurt. She deserves someone who will love and adore her, someone who won't break her.

My nerves are out of control as I wait for any sort of sign.

Maybe I'm asking too much. I could always force her hand by abdicating the throne. Then Gia and I could be free to do whatever we want, wherever we want.

Perhaps I should have gone that route. This childish game I'm about to play doesn't seem like a good idea anymore.

I'm about to call it off when Kiera smiles, setting hope alive once again. "I'm in."

Relief floods through me at those two simple words. "Thank you, Kiera."

"What all does this entail? I'm going to need a few more details than just fake dating."

I chuckle, glancing toward Simon to make sure he's still watching our interaction. The minute our eyes meet, he looks away. So obvious.

"A few staged appearances, giving her just enough to think her plan is working."

"Any kissing?" Her cheeks pink up slightly.

Forcing the smile, I try to soften the blow. "No, I can't do that to Gia."

"Oh," she says, scrunching her nose slightly. "I-I thought you two broke up."

I shake my head. "All for show. Which brings me to another point. Several of our staged dates will be at the Boar and Bull Pub."

"Okay?"

"Gia works there. We're using this as a double-edged sword, so to speak. My mother will think I'm rubbing this new relationship in her face, but it'll be a chance for me and Gia to see each other."

"I see." She mulls over my words. "Does Gia know about this."

90

"Yes." I cringe. "After much explaining and groveling, she understood."

Kiera gasps. "You mean you ambushed her yesterday with that breakup without telling her?"

I bite my lip. "Yes. Ow!"

She smacks my shoulder, hard, keeping a smile on her face to make it appear as if we're playing. "How could you do something so cruel?"

"I needed to make it seem real," I confess. "Not my proudest moment."

"I'd say not. Hopefully you made it up to her." This time it's my turn to blush. No words are needed as she gets the hint. "I see. Well, good for you two." She looks down before meeting my eyes again. "I'd really like to meet her. From what I saw at the gala, you really care for her."

"I do," I say, swallowing hard. "I love her."

Kiera brings a hand to her chest. "That's… I'm so happy for you, Lucien. Truly. Now I understand why this plan is so important. Anything I can do to keep you two together, I'm all in."

I lean over and kiss her cheek. This time not for show. "Thank you, Kiera."

CHAPTER
Eleven

Gia

The loud, annoying ring of my phone pulls me from one of the best dreams I've had all week. It was basically a non-stop sex marathon featuring Luke in all of his glory. And I do mean *all*. Even in my dreams that man rocks my world.

Unfortunately, the downside to having amazing sex dreams is waking up alone when you're extremely turned on and ready to go. Looks like it's going to be another morning of just me and my handheld showerhead again. As soon as I deal with whoever it is that decided to wake me up.

"Hello?" I grumble, leaving no mistake about how not awake I am.

"Oh goodness, Gia, you sound horrible. Are you ill?" Amelia asks in her quiet, demure voice.

I roll over onto my back, still blinking the sleep from my eyes. "No, just worked a long shift last night. What's up?"

"I was wondering if you'd be up for some shopping today."

Ugh, shopping. Not exactly what I wanted to do today. My plans focused more on making some nachos and binge watching whatever I could find on Netflix. With Luke out of town for the next few days, there's really nothing to look forward to, other than our secret chats and video calls. He had the foresight to get us unregistered phones so no one could track our movements or conversations.

But Amelia is one of my few friends here who still talks to me. Kendra is still giving me the silent treatment, even though Bryce, Connor, and I have pled my case to her.

"Sure, that sounds good," I lie. "What time were you thinking?"

"How fast can you get dressed?"

Oh, that soon. Looks like I'm going through the day as one very frustrated woman.

As much as I hate to admit it, this is exactly what I needed. A break from my tiny apartment where all I do is think about my current situation. In love with a man I can't formally be with because his mother hates me.

That's normal, right?

Amelia proudly swings the bags from her arms—at least the ones she decided not to have shipped to her house—while I walk next to her with my one bag containing a pair of jeans I couldn't pass up, even though she offered on several occasions to get me a few of the things I wanted.

My steps slow as we approach a familiar shop, one I haven't set foot in since the gala. Amelia senses my hesitation and turns around, practically dragging me by the arm inside.

"Amelia, I don't—"

"Nonsense. Everything will be fine. We're only going to pop in for a second so I can say hello to my dear sister-in-law."

Easy for her to say. She doesn't have a bullseye on the back of her head where Kendra is concerned.

A few people mill about inside the upscale boutique, sorting through the racks of high-end fashion while a few associates help them with their personal shopping. Despite Marguerite absolutely hating my guts, she's done wonders for Kendra's business. It's not often small retailers can compete with big corporate names. Her formal recommendation is better than any paid advertising.

I chew on my bottom lip as I scan the store, looking for any sign of its owner while weighing my potential exit strategies if she decides to throw me out.

"Kendra," Amelia calls as the woman herself appears from the back room. I quickly duck behind a mannequin, praying she didn't see me.

"Amelia, so good to see you." Kendra kisses her cheek and checks out her bags. "I see you've been busy this afternoon. Come to add to your collection?"

They both laugh but I can barely hear it above the rushing of blood through my ears. Not many things get me worked up. Heights—a little. Snakes—damn right. Spiders—burn everything down. Losing a friend then having to face them—I'd rather hold a spider while being chased by snakes after jumping out of a plane.

"Actually, I'm here on a mission."

Kendra quirks a brow. "Oh, do tell."

Unfortunately, my powers of invisibility don't work on Amelia as she waves me over. "It's a peace mission."

The minute Kendra lays eyes on me, her smile fades, turning into a scowl. "No."

She tries to turn away, but Amelia grabs her arm, halting her progress. "Please. For your favorite sister-in-law?"

Kendra rolls her eyes. "You're my only sister-in-law."

"All the more reason to say I'm the favorite." With her other hand, she grabs my arm and drags us to the back office. "Now, you two are going to talk and *listen* to what the other has to say. We're not leaving here until things are patched up." Geez, you'd think she was talking to two toddlers who got into a fight over a toy.

"It's not that simple," Kendra says.

"Only it is. I'm serious. No bloodshed, no destruction. Just open and honest discussion allowed." Amelia winks before shutting the door behind her. Suddenly I feel like a caged rabbit in the lion's den, waiting to be eaten. There's no way Kendra is going to magically forgive me. Not when she thinks I've betrayed her in the worst way possible.

"Look, obviously Amelia is not going to let us out of here until we hash this out," I start. "We can either do as she asks or pretend to make up and never have to see each other again."

Kendra sits at her desk while I occupy the chair in front of her. "The latter sounds good to me."

I sigh and fold my hands together, doing my best to stop them from shaking. "Kendra, you have to believe me. Nothing happened between me and Reid. I swear."

"The pictures suggest otherwise."

"From the media's point of view. You know how ruthless they can be, twisting the truth to fit their agenda. Do you know what those pictures have cost me?" She stares at me, unblinking. "Friendships that are priceless. Can I please explain?"

She waves a hand in front of her, still avoiding my eyes. "Go ahead."

I take a deep breath and blow it out slowly. This is it. She's either going to believe me or determine our relationship isn't worth salvaging. "That night, Luke and I were inseparable. I know you saw that. Everything was fine until he went into work mode, leaving me vulnerable to his mother's attacks. For whatever reason, she hates me and our relationship. She kept dropping little hints about how we would never last and that Kiera was his betrothed, that he was buying time by slumming it with me."

Kendra laughs. "Betrothed? You honestly fell for that?"

"I didn't know! For all I knew, that's how royal weddings are set up. A predetermined spouse to make the ultimate match and ensure a noble bloodline."

She laughs even more. "No one does that anymore. You watch too many movies."

"But it was what I believed. Marguerite played on my insecurities, letting it fester while keeping Luke occupied and away from me. Then Reid came over, extremely drunk, and asked for a dance." Her body goes rigid at the mention of his name. "I swear, Kendra, I didn't know he was going to kiss me. Hell, I didn't think he had feelings for me. He knew how Luke and I felt about each other. So when he pressed his lips to mine, I froze only briefly before shoving him away. I know how you feel about him and would *never* hurt you like that. Then Marguerite put her final dagger in my back as she pushed Luke and Kiera together and made me watch their interaction, telling me I should leave as fast as I can so I don't ruin his life. I had every intention to walk somewhere, but Reid offered to take me back to his place rather than sleeping on the streets. I was too tired and confused to argue. But I swear, nothing happened. Yes, I hugged him on his doorstep as I left the next morning, still wearing the ball gown from the night before. But that's it. Hand to God, I swear."

I can see the disbelief floating in her eyes. "Really? That's all you can come up with? I've heard better lies from my brothers."

"I know it sounds like I'm making excuses, but I'm not."

She narrows her eyes. "Why would the queen do such a thing? I've known her for years. She's not cruel like you're suggesting. Maybe it's your American skepticism clouding your judgment."

"Look, if you don't believe me, ask Luke himself. He knew about it before I did. We had been trying to lay low to avoid any unwanted attention. Unfortunately the whole evening played right into her hand." Kendra keeps her arms crossed firmly in front of her chest. Time to try another tactic. "Luke told me there would be a select number of photographers invited inside the gala."

"Right, to control what images could and could not be released."

I nod. "Now think about that statement. Who gives the approval for those photos? How could pictures of Reid and I get published unless *someone* allowed it?"

Finally, the first seed of doubt sprouts in her eyes. "But why?"

"That's the part I don't know," I say, shrugging my shoulders. "And who would have tipped off the paparazzi on where to find me the next morning? Or better yet, why would they care?"

I think that did it. Kendra stays quiet, mulling over all the information I've thrown at her. I know she has a close relationship with the queen, but she has to see the truth with everything laid in front of her.

"If you need confirmation, ask Bryce. He knows everything that's been going on."

Without a word, she pulls out her phone, tapping a few things on the screen before placing it on her desk. The ringing abruptly stops over the speaker as Bryce picks up.

"Oh, are you finally speaking to me?" Christ, not now. He can't piss her off, not when I'm so close to fixing things.

"Shut up and answer me one thing." She flicks her eyes to mine. "Is Gia telling the truth?"

Bryce stays quiet for a second. "What did she tell you?"

"That Marguerite is plotting against her, setting her up to keep her away from Luke. And Reid drunkenly kissed her."

I practically crawl out of my skin, willing Bryce to say the words. "It's all true."

Relief floods through my system as Kendra sits back in her chair. "But why?"

"That part we don't know," he says. "We're working on a plan to figure everything out. Gia, are you there?"

"Yeah, I'm here," I call out.

"Will you fill her in?"

I nod. "Of course."

"Good. Now maybe you can stop acting like a jackass toward Gia," he says, directing the comment at his twin.

"Love you too." She disconnects the call, plunging us back into silence. "Gia, I—"

I hold up a hand. "No need to say anything. I understand. I probably would have reacted the same way had the tables been turned."

She nods and places her folded hands on her desk. "So who is in on this plan?"

"Me and Luke, obviously. Reid, Bryce, Connor, Amelia, and Kiera."

"Kiera?" She draws her brows together. "What does she have to do with this?"

"She was being used as a pawn in the queen's game, so Luke thought she might want to help us get even."

"How do you know Kiera wasn't a willing participant? Not that I think she would be. She's the sweetest girl. A little sheltered and naïve, but you never know how people act when tempted with something they want." Guilt crosses her face again.

"Luke spoke with her the other day and she had no idea about the part she played in this whole mess. She also said she's willing to help Luke however she can because she saw how happy we were before everything went down."

Kendra's crestfallen face tugs at my heart. Her guilt is practically palpable, yet I don't hold anything against her. This is all on Marguerite for creating this chaos, not giving two shits about who she destroys in the process.

"I feel like such a fool. I know how much you care for Luke and vice versa. I don't know why I acted the way I did. Even before the gala, I had suspicions about you and Reid. Jealousy drove me mad because I've wished for years that he'd look at me the way he looked at you. And I knew deep down you only saw him as a friend." Her eyes fill with unshed tears. "Can you ever forgive me?"

"Of course," I say, abandoning my chair to wrap my arms around her. "I was afraid you'd never speak to me again."

She softly laughs. "It's a good thing I have a pushy sister-in-law."

Speaking of. Three knocks sound on the door before Amelia pushes it open. "I didn't hear any furniture flying around so I assume things are safe?"

I laugh and swipe a finger under my eyes, catching a few tears that leaked out. "Battle zone is clear."

Amelia darts her gaze between us, verifying that we are still intact, and no blood was shed. "About time." She takes up the chair next to me with a smile. "Now, let's discuss the next phase in the plan."

"Which is?" Apparently she knows more than I do. You'd think it would be the other way around, but when Luke calls me at night, talking isn't exactly a high priority. At least not *that* kind of talking.

A slow smirk creeps across her lips. "A chance meeting."

Kendra tilts her head. "With whom?"

"Clearly you two aren't thinking correctly." She blows out a frustrated breath. "A chance meeting between Luke and Gia while Kiera is in tow."

Oh. That plan. Nothing about that plan is appealing to me. Yes, I know it's for the greater good, but I don't want to see the man who holds my heart press up against someone else or pretend to show her any sort of affection.

It's all a show.

I'm going to need plenty of reminders to not go insane.

Matt was kind enough to give me a Saturday night off with only a day's notice. Through a lack of options, I had to divulge our plan, which now makes him an accessory to possible treason. Luke says otherwise, but he has nothing to fear since it's his mother. Even though Matt was a bit skeptical at first, once he found out all the awful things Marguerite has been doing, he was more than on board. The last thing I ever wanted to do was bad mouth Luke's mom, but really, she started it.

Childish? Maybe a little.

"Where are we going exactly?" I put the finishing touches on my eyeliner after being forced to change my outfit four times.

"You'll see," Amelia chirps from her perch on the couch.

Both she and Kendra have been quiet about the plan. Something about needing to know and natural surprise.

I stopped listening after the tenth time of the same answer.

Once my simple outfit of leather pants that I can barely breathe in, heels I'm certain to sprain an ankle in—thanks to Kendra—and some off-the-shoulder way-too-sexy top was approved, we slide into the back of the car Amelia rented for us and head downtown, stopping in front of some swanky upscale club.

Not what I was expecting.

Loud, thundering music bounces off the walls, vibrating through my chest as we make our way to the back roped-off area.

Almost reminds me of the clubs from back home. Only less beer and pot smell. In fact, I'm not even sure they serve beer here since almost every single person is holding either a martini glass or lowball filled with some amber liquid.

"You made it," Connor says, standing from the table as we approach. I flash a quick smile before he kisses his wife, thankfully keeping it somewhat chaste. Us single people don't like to watch couples make out.

Though I guess technically I'm not single. But I get to pretend while watching the man I love fawn over another woman.

Fuck, I need a drink.

Connor kisses my cheek. "Wow, you look amazing tonight."

Hmm, I wonder if I can even sit in these pants. They're practically cutting off the circulation to my legs as it is.

"Thanks."

Bryce must notice my dilemma because he stands next to me, engulfing me in a huge hug. "You're really not going to show any mercy, are you?"

"Mercy?"

He smacks his forehead before flagging down a waitress. "Oh, right. You're in the dark. Sorry."

A tall, leggy blonde wearing a skimpy black outfit saunters up to the table. "What can I get for you?" She eyes up Reid, who hasn't budged an inch since we arrived, keeping his eyes trained on the rest of us.

"I'll have a cosmopolitan," Amelia says, clinging to her husband.

"Same," says Kendra.

"Whiskey on the rocks," Connor says.

"Bourbon, neat," Reid says, finally showing some sign of life.

"Vodka martini." Figures Bryce would be different.

"And you?" She looks at me impatiently.

"Three fingers of whatever top-shelf whiskey you have, neat please." I'll probably regret this in the morning, but something tells me I'm also going to want to forget most of tonight.

Once the drinks arrive and the slow burn of the whiskey quiets the riot building inside me, I finally start to relax.

"Good evening."

Spoke too soon. Every hair on the back of my neck stands on end and I've never been more thankful for a padded bra in my life as my nipples tighten painfully at the smooth sound of his voice.

So much for relaxing.

"Luke!" Kendra loudly proclaims, sliding away from the bench to throw her arms around him.

The butterflies in my stomach swarm and flutter as I look him up and down. God, he's practically edible in his dress pants and shirt sleeves rolled to his elbows. The only thing that would complete the look would be his glasses, but I know he only wears them for me.

"Kiera, you look lovely," Kendra says, hugging her as well.

I hardly noticed her since I couldn't drag my gaze away from Luke. Her blonde hair is pulled neatly into some fancy updo and the expensive-looking dress hugs all her curves, accentuating her best assets. None of it matters. Her arm is hooked through Luke's, draping along his side as if she belongs there.

No wonder they wouldn't tell me what's going on tonight. They needed an honest reaction. Well, they got it.

"Thank you." Her demure voice is sweet and quiet, something expected of a lady with a noble pedigree. Unlike my sailor mouth and American accent. We couldn't be more opposite if we tried. She turns to me and genuinely smiles. "I don't think we've been formally introduced. I'm Kiera Wagner." She holds her well-manicured hand out. Part of me questions if this is a real gesture or something for the newly acquired crowd down below since *his royal highness* stepped foot in the club. Now the balcony seat makes sense. It gives everyone a good look at our interactions, keeping us secluded while still in the public eye.

Her smile starts to slip, so I place my hand in hers. "Gia Hartley. Pleasure to meet you."

"Likewise. I've heard so much about you."

Lord knows from whom.

Even though I know it's all for show, it doesn't stop the ache forming in my heart as she places a hand on Luke's chest. Lights flash down below, knowing how juicy of a story this is going to make tomorrow.

Time to shine.

"You two need to catch up." I flag our waitress down so Luke and Kiera can order their drinks. Luke keeps his eyes trained on some imaginary spot on the wall, not once glancing my way. I'm sure if he did, we'd give everything away and we can't afford to do that.

After another round, my body starts to relax and loosen. It finally starts to feel like old times as the guys rip on each other and us girls giggle and snicker over the stupidity of men.

"Time to dance," Amelia proclaims, grabbing my hand and gingerly dragging me from my seat. Damn, I just got comfortable.

Kendra and Kiera follow behind, leaving the men to stare as we make our way down the stairs to the packed dance floor. The music is ten times louder down here, drowning out my thoughts and clearing my head. I needed this more than I knew. A moment not to dwell on Luke and our current fucked-up situation.

I let the music take over, swaying my body to the beat and ignoring the throbbing in my feet. Not sure why I'm the only one dressed in leather when everyone else gets to be in a dress. Whatever. I make this shit look hot.

After a few songs, Bryce and Reid join us on the floor while Connor and Luke look on from the balcony. I drag my hair off my shoulders, wishing I'd had the foresight to put it up like Kiera, who still looks cool and put together. Then again, she's not wearing a sweatbox for clothes.

"Dance with me," Bryce yells over the loud music, bringing a smile to my face.

"Only if you can keep up."

A wicked gleam twinkles in his eyes as he puts on his best moves. Wow, I'm impressed. He twirls me around the floor with ease, even dropping us low without getting stuck—which at this point in the night is no short feat.

Reid taps on Bryce's shoulder. "Hey, my turn," he says,

taking my hands and bringing me close. My whole body goes on alert, remembering what happened the last time we shared a dance. "Relax. It's all a show, remember?"

He went from not meeting my eyes to pressing his hips against mine in no time. "My brain understands, but my heart is having second thoughts."

His hot breath tickles my ear. "The endgame is worth it." The sensual beat creates a hunger deep inside as Reid continues to hold me close, dancing like we're the only two on the floor. He does a quick turn, giving me a full view of the balcony and its occupants. "See, this is what people are looking at."

No one can miss Luke's scowl, or the V permanently etched between his brows. He's... jealous?

"I thought the game was to play it up for the queen."

Reid runs his hands up my back. "You're not the only one that's been kept in the dark about tonight. We didn't know if you two could play the part without falling all over each other. The paparazzi know real emotion from fake. Right now, you both are selling it. See?"

A camera flashes, capturing Reid and I dancing while turning its lens to Luke, who quickly leaves his perch to descend the stairs.

"I think it's working," Amelia says, stealing Reid from my grip before twirling him around, directly into Kendra's arms.

Looks like I'm not the only one getting played here. Amelia throws me a wink while crooking a finger to her husband, beckoning him to come down.

Another pair of hands slide over my hips. "Hey gorgeous. Care for a dance?" the stranger asks as I turn to face him. He's good-looking. Clean shaven, slightly taller than me in these heels, and friendly dark brown eyes.

"Sure, why not."

We sway to the beat as Luke quickly crosses the floor, his eyes trained on the hands at my hips. Kiera notices and intercepts him, pulling him close.

I can't stop staring as she runs her hands up his chest, toying with the hair above his ear until a slow smile crosses his lips.

"What's your name, beautiful?"

Forcing myself to look at the stranger, I smile and turn on the charm. "Gia. You?"

"Richard. Are you here with friends tonight?"

I nod. "They decided I needed a night out."

His smile would melt the panties off a typical woman, but not for me. It's all wrong. He's just a pretty face. Nothing more.

"I'm glad."

The song switches and I catch a glimpse of Luke over Kiera's shoulder. His eyes burn into mine, sending heat coursing through my veins until I'm afraid I'll pass out.

I pull back from Richard, who raises a brow. "Sorry, have to make a pit stop. Be right back."

Not giving him the chance to respond, I quickly dart off the floor, making a beeline to the restrooms in the back corner, locking myself in the first available stall.

Geez, you'd think with all the sweating I've done, these leather pants would be easy to get off. Now my only concern is getting them back on without having a Ross Geller crisis from *Friends*.

The stars must have aligned because I was able to slide them up and down without issue. I grab a paper towel and run it under some cold water, pressing it against my heated skin, mindful not to touch my face. The last thing I need is my makeup to melt off.

Kiera walks through the door as I fix my hair, our eyes meeting in the mirror. "Gia, look, I want you to know that I'm sorry about everything."

I ball up the used paper towel and toss it in the trash. "You have nothing to be sorry for. It's all part of the game, right?"

She takes a step forward. "Yes, but it can't be easy for you both. It's why I had to stop Luke before he blew our cover on the dance floor."

"You saw that too." Had she not stepped in, I'm positive Luke would have decked the guy and that would make the headlines rather than his new relationship. I lean against the sink and cross my arms over my chest. "This sucks."

"It really does." Kiera cracks a smile while placing a hand on my forearm. "Please know that no matter what you see, it's not real. I know Luke's feelings toward you and would never interfere. He's too dear a friend and I only want his happiness."

I cover her hand with mine and force a smile. "Can you try to not make it too believable?"

She nods. "I'll see what I can do."

Once we leave the restroom, Kiera makes her way back to everyone else while I head back up to the balcony, watching the crowd below. Kendra's now dancing with Bryce, who twirls her ridiculously fast around the floor.

I flag down our waitress, downing another glass of whiskey, praying the burn will numb the events of the night. Reid slides in next to me, draping his arm across the back of the booth.

"It's funny. When I first got here, you wouldn't even look at me. Now you're acting like we're a couple."

He sheepishly looks over and shrugs. "We sort of have to pretend we are. I was too nervous in the beginning because I wasn't sure how you'd react."

Great. Another performance. I quickly finish my drink and order another. "Wonderful."

"Don't act like it's a chore to be nice to me."

I swing my eyes to him and scowl. "Look, I'm dealing with a lot right now. A little slack from you would be appreciated. Unless you want a reminder of why we have to do this in the first place."

Shit. I didn't mean to say that. Sure, Reid had a hand in our current situation, but he's still an innocent bystander.

"Look, Gia…"

I shake my head and place a hand on his leg. "I'm sorry. I didn't mean that. You've been a good friend and I'm a little drunk and frustrated." Finishing off the new drink, I lay my head against his shoulder and sigh. "This will work, right? We won't have to do this forever?"

He leans his head against mine. "It will work."

After a few hours, the club starts to clear out as the house lights take over the neon ones.

"Looks like that's our cue," Kendra says, stretching her arms above her head. I've had enough alcohol that I'm not sure I can even blink normally. Or at all.

Amelia turns my way, noticing my current state. "I'll need some help with this one."

Several hands help lift me up from the comfy booth. I have no idea who they belong to. Nor do I care. All I want is my bed and to get out of these pants. And Luke, but two out of three will have to do.

Somehow I manage not to kill myself while walking up the creaky wooden steps to my apartment, even managing to find the lock on the first try.

I kick the heels off, not caring about where they land. I'll clean up tomorrow. I strip out of my shirt with ease on my way to the bedroom. The pants are proving a little more difficult, forcing me to hop on one foot while bracing myself against the wall. Leather and alcohol do not go well together.

Another tug sends me off-balance, setting a collision course—face-first—for the floor. Only a pair of arms wrap around my waist, halting me midair. His glorious scent washes over me, turning my muscles and bones into Jell-O.

"You're a mess," he says with no amusement in his voice.

"Less judgment and more help."

This time I get a chuckle from him as he scoops me up and sets me gingerly on the bed. I fall back almost immediately and lift my hips as he tugs the horrendous material off my body.

"What should I do with these?"

I lift onto my elbows, narrowing my eyes at the offending garment.

"Burn them."

Luke tosses them to the floor. "Maybe not right away. I have a few ideas for them first." He helps me under the covers, stripping down himself before crawling in behind me.

"Isn't it dangerous for you to be here?" I run my fingers over his arms holding on to me as if I'll disappear.

His lips find my shoulder, trailing kisses along the slope to my ear. "I needed to see you. To hold you. To be next to you."

"Tonight sucked," I say through a yawn.

He nods and pulls me closer. "Agreed."

"Let's not do this again. No more secret ambushes. We need to be in on the plans from now on."

He kisses me again. "Also agreed."

I turn in his arms and run my fingers through his hair, trailing down his cheeks before resting on the side of his neck. "I don't know if I can do this. It's harder than I thought."

The moment our lips connect, every worry and fear disappear. This is the reason we're torturing ourselves. A few hours of pain for a lifetime of happiness.

"Let's not think about it. I just want to hold you in my arms and tell you that I love you."

I rest my cheek against his chest, feeling his heartbeat soothe my soul. "I love you, too."

Once our breathing regulates and slows, I fall into the darkness, hoping to see the light when I wake up.

CHAPTER
Twelve

Luke

"Wonderful," I mutter under my breath, cringing internally as the paper crinkles in my grip. There, plastered on the front page of some cheap tabloid magazine, is a picture of me and Kiera dancing at the club the other night with a smaller picture of Gia snuggled up to Reid in the corner.

Bachelor prince off the market? Former American flame found in the arms of best friend.

As much as I hate this, I know it's the lesser of two evils. Playing to the paparazzi is just as important as playing to my mother. It doesn't make it any easier to read the headlines or look at the pictures, only to gut me as people whisper and gossip about things they don't need to be involved in. My love life is nobody's business, though I'm the only one who sees it that way.

Poor Gia and Reid. Their names are being drug through the mud in this whole scandal. I know Reid said he was okay with the consequences, calling it his penance for the night of the gala and the weeks leading up to it, but it's too much.

"Lucien," Mother calls in her fake voice, almost like nails on a chalkboard. "Is it true what they're saying in the papers?"

I promptly toss the offending article in the trash receptacle next to my desk. "You of all people should know not to listen to gossip rags."

She elegantly sits in the chair opposite me, folding her hands and resting them on her knees, smiling like the cat who ate the canary. "Is it gossip if it's the truth? I hate to say I told you so, but—"

"Then don't."

"There's no need to be rude, Lucien." She adjusts the hem of her skirt, brushing away an invisible piece of lint. "It's wonderful to see you and Kiera getting along so swimmingly. Surely you must know this match is better suited than that *American* girl."

It takes everything I have not to storm out of the room and away from my royal duties. The nerve of her thinking she knows what's best for me or that she has any authority to rule over my life. But this is all part of the game. Instead, I school my features, giving nothing away.

"I guess it all worked out in the end." If only she knew the true meaning of the statement.

She seems appeased with this information, standing with a nod and straightening her dress. "Well, I've invited both Kiera and her parents to dinner tonight to celebrate this newfound union."

Fuck. There go my plans to meet up with Gia later. Looks like it'll be a late-night trip instead.

I nod and turn my attention to Nick as he saunters through the door.

"Nicolai, darling. I'm so glad you're back." She sweeps him into her arms and kisses his cheek. "How was your trip?"

He smiles, pride clearly showing across his face. "Excellent. We procured another four locations and millions of dollars in donations."

"That's wonderful." She places a loving hand on his cheek.

A knock at my office door turns our heads as Thomas steps through. "Pardon the interruption, Your Majesty, but your morning meeting is here early."

One thing Mother loves is punctuality, though twenty minutes early may be a bit much.

She slips on her mask, poising herself as the regal dignitary she is, never once letting her annoyance show. "Very good, Thomas. Thank you."

Without another glance my way, she places a hand on Nick's cheek and follows Thomas out of my office. She doesn't try to hide who her favorite child is. Nick, on the other hand, isn't amused as he rolls his eyes and takes her vacated seat.

"Could she be more obvious?"

I shrug and sit back in my leather chair. "The golden boy has returned. Maybe now she'll get off my back for a while."

Nick chuckles and unbuttons his suit coat. "And what has Mother Dearest done now?"

Has he been living under a rock? How does he not know of the torment she's determined to inflict on me? Then again, he left right after the gala for this foundation business, without saying a word to anyone.

Knowing a picture is worth a thousand words, I dig the offending newspaper from the waste bin and toss it across my desk. "This."

His eyes widen as he reads the headlines. "What? No, this

can't be right. You and Kiera? Since when? And Gia and Reid? What on earth have I missed?"

"Brace yourself, brother. You're in for a wild ride."

I spare no details of Mother's deceit, starting from the night of the gala and all the pain and suffering Gia and I have endured at her hands. Finally, I lay down the plan, hoping he'll see my side and agree it's the only option when taking on the viper.

"Damn," he says with a whistle. "What is her problem?"

"Your guess is as good as mine. From what I can gather, her plan is to have Kiera and I wed to bring our two families together."

"I wonder if her father is aware of this."

Count Wagner is a cunning man. Nothing gets by him. "It's hard to believe he'd be taken for a fool. I'd bet my inheritance he's in on the plot."

"But why is she after you? I'm unmarried and she's never once said a word on it." Nick props his foot on his knee.

"Because you're the favorite and do everything she asks. I'm sure she expects you to fall into line if she said you were to marry someone of her choosing."

His face turns ashen, like he swallowed a bitter pill. "I'm not sure about that."

"Please," I say, leaning back again. "As heir apparent, you have everything at your feet. Not to mention you haven't been labeled the playboy prince, even though it's hardly the truth."

He laughs and I want to punch him. "It's not my fault you always ended up photographed with different women at every function."

"Because I'm a nice guy and was helping them with their modeling careers. Do you know how much of a boost they got just by being seen with me?"

Nick raises a brow. "Ego much?"

I roll my eyes. "Fuck off. You know as well as I do it's all about who you know, not what you know. A surefire way to get in the spotlight is to be photographed with a celebrity. People will automatically flock to you, search you up online, and beg you to cover events you'd been denied previously."

"Such a philanthropist."

"Smart-ass."

"Besides, none of those women hold a candle to Gia."

Nick stays quiet for a moment before leaning forward and resting his elbows on his knees. "Why go through all of this for her?"

I tilt my head to the side, not understanding his question. "Why not?"

He sighs and keeps his eyes on mine. "Explain it to me."

How do you put feelings into words and do them justice? "Gia is the air I breathe. She brought me back to life when I was dead inside, going through the motions as if I was on autopilot. I crave her wit, her humor. Hell, even her mannerisms, obnoxious as they are. She's a bright light in a dark tunnel and I can't help being pulled to her." I can't help the smile as I think about her. "She's my match, my guiding star... my everything."

Nick nods, a grin tugging at his lips. "Then you're doing the right thing. Maybe doing it the hard way, but it's still right. Mother will never accept her unless she has a reason to. It's clear your happiness isn't a high priority. This way, you're forcing her hand."

"Exactly." Thank God he understands. If he couldn't take my side, I don't know what I'd do. Even though I'm willing to go this alone, having another person in my corner, especially family, always helps.

"Here, let me add some ammunition to your arsenal."

I quirk a brow. "What do you mean?"

He straightens up, taking a more serious note with his posture. This isn't Nick anymore—my fun-loving brother. No, this is Nicolai—his business side, the one commanding the room to get deals finalized. If I didn't know him better, I'd almost be afraid.

"I've been trying to find a way to talk to you since the gala. There's something important we need to discuss." When I don't respond, he swallows hard. "Hopefully this won't affect your plans."

A bout of nerves collects in my stomach, practically making the organ sink into my shoes. "What did you do?"

CHAPTER
Thirteen

Gia

"**G**ia! Another ale," one of the regulars yells across the bar. Work has been my only saving grace during this whole ordeal. After the club incident, Luke and I have barely had any time to talk, let alone get together. His impromptu sleepover that night was cut short due to keeping the plan. Waking up alone, seeing the dent in his pillow and the empty space brought me to tears. And his foundation work has been keeping him busier than ever. Add in the work he does for the crown and we might as well be passing strangers. A few times I've caught myself staring at his picture in a Google search or on the alerts I have set up every time his name gets mentioned in an article.

I miss the ease of our relationship. I miss the Luke I met back in Chicago, when everything was simple.

It's slow tonight, only a dozen or so people occupying the tables and stools. Matt needed the night off, leaving me to fend for myself, so it's probably best there's a small crowd. Not that I wouldn't be able to handle a packed house. I've done it before. It's all a matter of making them come to you. And it helps that we don't serve food. The more I can stay behind the bar, the better.

The door opens, drawing my curiosity for a moment as I clean up a few abandoned tables.

"Look who it is," Reid says, smiling widely. Bryce and Connor follow behind him, sporting equal grins.

Oh thank God. My night just got better. Maybe Luke will show up. It's odd to see the three out without their fourth.

Reid engulfs me in a hug, which I half-heartedly return. With everything going on, I don't know if this is part of the act or if it's real. But the contact is still welcome either way. Bryce and Connor follow suit, calming my mind even more.

"Hey guys. I'm so glad you're here." They walk to the bar and take up the empty seats in front of the taps while I place their usual drinks in front of them. "What's up with you guys?"

"Just needed a night out," Connor says, taking a sip from his mug.

"And to see your pretty face," Reid adds, causing me to blush slightly.

I wipe my hands on the bar rag and roll my eyes. "Whatever. I look like a hot mess tonight. Apparently, I've forgotten how to hold on to things and spilled at least three drinks on myself." Luckily, my apron absorbed most of the mess, although this is the last clean apron I found in the back, so if I have any more accidents, I'm on my own.

"You're still beautiful," says Bryce. "It's why we keep coming here."

Oh Lord. "Save your charms for an unattached girl. They don't work on me."

He laughs and leans forward. "Can't blame a guy for trying."

With them here, it helps to quickly pass the time. Between the jokes and laughs and the other customers, two hours fly by in a blink. Not to mention my service got better with my mood lightened. And I haven't had an accident. All the glassware has stayed intact.

The door opens and I turn to smile at the new guest, but shock replaces joy as the drink in my hand crashes to the ground in slow motion.

I don't know why I'm shocked to see him. He comes in almost every night, sitting in the back corner nursing one drink and keeping an eagle eye on me.

Simon.

Reid pointed him out the first time he showed up, giving me a warning to be on my toes. Marguerite must not be convinced things are working in her favor if she keeps sending him to spy on me. Or she really loves to torture me.

It could go either way.

The guys notice him as well, putting an instant scowl on their faces.

"Bloody hell, can't you get one night away from this guy?" Connor says, tracking Simon all the way to his usual table in the back.

For the queen's spy, he sure does make it obvious. If I wanted to stay incognito, I'd blend in with the crowd. Join them not isolate myself to draw attention.

Then again, he probably doesn't want to stay hidden. He wants his presence known, egging me on until I screw up.

Not a chance. I'm in this game to win.

Reid reaches across the bar and squeezes my hand. "Showtime."

I mutter under my breath, "I guess."

So much for my good mood. But I plaster on my best smile, drawing from my stage experience when I was in sixth grade, and play my part of Reid's... whatever.

It's the performance of the night; leaning against the bar, laughing at every single thing he says, brushing my fingers across his back as I serve the tables, even sitting on his leg when I'm "on a break".

Simon keeps his eyes on me, doing his usual creepy stalker stare, following my every move.

Midnight finally comes around and I've never been so excited for bar close.

"Sorry, guys, but it's time to go," I announce to the few stragglers still nursing their drinks. They grunt in disapproval and empty their glasses, tossing money on the counter before heading out the door. Leaving Reid, Bryce, Connor... and Simon.

"Hey, Simon, time to pack it up," Reid yells over his shoulder.

He smirks and brings his half-full glass to the bar, sliding it and a few bills my way.

"Keep the change." I watch him walk out the door, taking with him every ounce of tension I was carrying in my shoulders.

"God, I hate him." I quickly walk to the door and turn the lock. "One night, that's all I ask."

I take a seat on one of the empty stools and rest my head on top of my folded arms, trying hard to turn my brain off.

"Gia, everything will be fine," Bryce says, rubbing my back.

I just can't see it anymore. When I looked to the future, it was always me and Luke raising a family, going on vacations together, doing normal things. Yes, I understand it was a pipe dream considering his role and occupation. Normal isn't in his vocabulary. But somewhere there must be some semblance of it. No one can be expected to work all day long and never be themselves.

I sit up and stare at the wall. Tears well in my eyes as I try not to think. "It's just... so hard right now. I haven't spoken to Luke in what feels like forever. My every move is being watched like I'm some criminal. And to top it all off, I have to pretend to be someone I'm not." I turn to Reid and weakly smile. "No offense."

"None taken," he says, resting a hand on my arm. "You don't deserve this."

"Have you read the papers? I'm the American harlot who used the prince to get her way, only to leave him heartbroken and straight into the arms of a better match." A hot tear slowly treks down my cheek. "I just wish I knew what I ever did to Marguerite for her to hate me so much."

"It's not you," Connor says, leaning past his brother to catch my eyes. "She's hated every single girl Luke has ever shown interest in. The only person she ever wanted him to marry was Kiera. This isn't personal."

I walk behind the bar and pour myself a heavy-handed vodka tonic, greedily gulping it down. "Feels kind of personal when she sends her lackey to watch my every move or allows the papers to say what they want about me."

As I make another drink for myself, Reid takes his phone out of his pocket and types out a quick message. Not wanting to drink alone, I refill their glasses. After all, misery loves company.

Between the four of us, it hardly takes any time to clean and finish the closing routine. Connor pays for their tab—despite my objections—as they put their stools up on the bar counter.

"Hey, let's plan a vacation soon. We're due for a little relaxation away from everything."

Ironic that I'm here on a vacation and I'm in desperate need of one. "Getting away sounds heavenly. Just let me know where and when so I can give Matt a heads-up."

"I'll have Kendra work on it since she's a better planner than us," Bryce says.

I laugh and give him a hug. "Probably for the best otherwise we'd end up camping again."

"Hey, camping isn't so bad," Connor says.

"Excluding this year." Reid's somber tone pulls at my heart.

"It wasn't all bad." I give him a hug. "We had some laughs and that's better than nothing."

My comment cheers him up slightly. "I suppose." He gives the brothers a pointed look and nods toward the door. "We better get out of your hair so you can get out of here."

With our final goodbyes and a few more hugs, they leave me alone to finish counting out the till. Boring and monotonous as it is, it calms my mind to focus on something else.

I'm filling out my drop sheet when a pair of arms wrap around my waist, sending my heart catapulting out of my chest and setting off my fighting instincts as I jab an elbow directly into the person's side as hard as I can.

On shaky feet, I quickly turn around, ready to take on my unknown assailant but freeze when I see Luke clutching his ribs while trying to keep a smile on his face.

"What the—Luke! You scared the shit out of me," I cry out, smacking his shoulder several times. His tousled dark hair looks like he's done nothing but run his hands through it for the last few hours. But those sexy blue eyes staring me down behind his glasses ignites a fire inside me.

He laughs and pulls me to his side, bending slightly to claim my lips in a heated, passionate kiss. One mixed with longing and need, like a couple who hasn't seen each other in days. I wrap my arms around his neck and pull him close, convinced there's still space between us even though I have nowhere else to go.

We break apart, panting and out of breath. "Wha-what are you doing here?"

Luke tucks a piece of hair behind my ear and kisses the spot behind it. "I was informed you were struggling today." His warm breath creates a swarm of goose bumps across my skin, not to mention a sudden need and desire between my legs. "I'm here for you, angel."

"I've missed you." I snuggle into his embrace, desperately clinging to him for fear he'll disappear any moment.

He sets me on a stool and occupies the one next to it, pulling me closer to run his hands up and down my thighs. "Tell me, what's troubling you?"

I huff out a breath. "Simon was in again."

Red slowly creeps up Luke's neck. "Fucking hell. When will she leave us alone?"

"I asked the same thing." I stifle a sob threatening to break through. No, I won't cry over this. She doesn't get my pain, my tears, my heartache. "It was just the icing on my day."

"Angel." His palm warms my cheek and I lean into his touch, letting him try to wash away all the bad feelings and fears from my mind. "What do you need?"

His eyes bore into mine, tearing apart every defense I have. I don't know when it happened, but he's become my whole world. Nothing matters when I'm in his arms. All our troubles disappear like a thief in the night.

I break down and cup his cheeks with both hands, the first tear slowly leaking from my eyes. "You. Only you."

Luke sweeps me into his arms, plundering my mouth with

his, our tongues swirling and fighting for dominance. All these lonely nights have made me crave him more. I don't know why I let these negative thoughts in my head, let the newspaper articles bother me when I know they're false.

"Talk to me," he pleads between kisses, floating his fingers from my face to my neck, constantly keeping us in contact.

"It's stupid." He's not impressed with the brush-off, not that I expected him to be. "Fine. Seeing these articles claiming your pairing with Kiera is one for the ages irritates me. Then Simon always shows up, creepily staring from the back corner. And, to add insult to injury, he doesn't even tip well."

Luke's face softens. Not mockingly or with pity, but empathy because he knows what this is doing to me—to us. It can't be any easier for him.

"Ignore them. We both know what's true. Everything else doesn't matter."

"Easier said than done," I say. "You don't have patrons giving their condolences for losing the most eligible bachelor on the face of the planet, according to them."

Luke twists his lips to the side before leaning forward, skimming them down the column of my throat, dipping his tongue in the hollow spot, knowing what it does to me.

"They don't know what they're talking about." Those evil lips continue their descent as he unbuttons my shirt to gain more access. "The most eligible bachelor isn't eligible anymore." He nips the sensitive flesh of my breast, pulling back the cup to reveal my pert nipple. The first swipe of his tongue nearly has me falling off the stool. "He's madly in love with a smart, sexy bartender who is unlike any other woman he's ever met. No one holds a candle to her." I let out a moan as his lips close around the aching bud, sucking and biting, trying to drive me mad with desire.

"Luke." Everything inside me begs for release as he continues his ministrations, mimicking his movements on my other breast with his free hand.

"Are you still working?"

Work? Oh, fuck. I completely forgot I'm still on the clock. Thankfully I balanced my till and only need to put the money in the safe.

"Yeah," I pant out.

With all the effort I possess, I push him away, barely covering myself up while I gather everything together. Luke trails behind me, keeping his hands on my breasts while pressing into my back. The seventy or so feet to the office take a lifetime. All I want to do is grind my ass on his impressive erection and shed every piece of clothing we own.

Once everything is secured and locked up, Luke pounces, attacking my mouth and body with a need I haven't seen.

"Let's go upstairs." Somehow I form a coherent sentence as I palm his straining cock through his jeans, eliciting a moan from deep within his throat.

My back hits the door, our mouths still moving in tandem. He pulls back and I giggle at his fogged-up glasses and swollen red lips.

"Angel, I want nothing more than to take you upstairs and show you how much you mean to me, but I can't stay the night."

Right. The arrangement.

I rub the spot above my heart, feeling the familiar ache form inside my chest.

"Oh." I try to keep the disappointment from my voice but fail miserably.

Luke tilts my chin up, running his fingers through my hair before wrapping his hand around the back of my neck. "We're going to my place instead."

His place? "But… how?"

Without a word, he buttons up my shirt and takes my hand, leading me to the employee lot where Reid's car is parked.

"We have a getaway car."

Luke opens the passenger door for me, placing a kiss on my lips before running around and climbing in the other side. He pops open the glove box and takes out a familiar baseball hat, securing it firmly on his head.

I smirk. "Cubs, huh?"

He grabs my hand and kisses the back of it. "I have a thing for Chicago."

Smooth. Very smooth.

We pull out of the lot and head toward his place, completely incognito under the veil of darkness. Not a soul is around as he drives through the back gates where the public doesn't have direct access. He parks the car directly in front of his house, wrapping an arm around my waist as we stroll through the door like it was a normal occurrence.

I haven't been back here since the whole gala incident and am thankful he doesn't live inside the palace, just in the complex. This is about as close to his mother as I ever want to be. I only hope he's sure his house staff has their loyalties straight.

The minute his heavy bedroom door shuts, he turns the lock with heated eyes, undressing me until I'm practically naked. Far be it from me to go against his desires.

Slowly, I thread each button through the hole, teasing him as I walk backward toward his bed. Luke doesn't move, only watches with rapt attention as the shirt falls from my shoulders, turning my attention to my jeans, drawing them slowly down my legs until they join the discarded shirt.

My bra strap slips down my shoulder as I crawl onto the

giant bed, settling in the middle with my legs spread wide open. "Wanna help me?" With both straps now hanging down, I palm my breasts, feeling their weight in my hands as I squeeze them and moan.

Luke stalks toward me, his eyes dark like a hunter looking for his prey. The Cubs hat flies across the room with a flick of his wrist—along with his glasses—keeping his gaze trained on my hands. Next, he pulls the shirt over his head. I can't stop staring as his abs flex and contract, how his chest expands with each breath, unless my gaze lands on that glorious V peeking above the waistband of his jeans. I lick my lips in anticipation.

"Want something, angel?" His amused tone makes me squeeze a little harder, pinching a nipple between two fingers. I moan as he drags the zipper down, never once breaking eye contact as the denim hits the floor. Unable to resist, I let my eyes wander downward and I'm rewarded with the most amazing prize ever.

His hard cock bobbing under its own weight, fully ready to take me on.

I love it when he goes commando.

Without warning, he pounces, spreading me wide across the bed, ripping the bra in two, along with my panties. Need rushes through me, leaving me wet and ready for everything to come.

"You're amazing," he says, replacing my hands with his. I arch my back off the bed when his lips encircle one of my nipples, biting down just hard enough to send a pulse racing between my legs.

He takes his time, torturing me with his lips and tongue, making me writhe with need.

Fuck this. I don't have the patience for foreplay tonight.

I lean up and capture his lips. At the same time, I wrap a

hand around his straining cock, pumping him a few times while twisting at the head. He hisses through his teeth and it's all I need. I push him onto his back, quickly straddling his hips before sinking on top of him, relishing in the feeling as he's fully seated inside me.

"Fuck, Gia," he moans, throwing his head back when I start to move. I've become a master at reading his body, knowing what turns him on and what moves keep it lasting all night. He grabs one of my bouncing tits, circling a nipple with his tongue as I angle my body closer, alternating between shallow and deep thrusts.

The familiar build-up inside me begs for release as my breast pops from his mouth. Changing the angle again, I lean back to brace my hands on his shins. Luke takes advantage and presses a thumb against my clit, practically making me see stars.

I moan and ride his cock like we have all the time in the world. Nothing from outside those doors can touch us. Not here, not like this.

The orgasm takes me by surprise as I shudder and struggle to maintain my momentum. Luke seizes the opportunity and flips me over, pushing between my shoulder blades while leaving my ass sticking up in the air. He plunges in hard, taking no prisoners with each welcome thrust. The sound of slapping skin mixes with our moans and prayers echoing off the walls.

My control wanes as he leans forward, taking an earlobe between his teeth. "Who do you belong to?" he grunts, grabbing a fistful of hair to pull me back so our eyes lock.

"Y-you," I pant, loving the mixture of pain and pleasure.

He hits a deep spot inside me, and my eyes practically roll into the back of my head. "And who do I belong to?"

How does he expect me to talk when all I want to do is scream and cry and beg him never to stop?

"M-me."

Luke hums in satisfaction, keeping his grip on my hair while holding my arms behind my back for leverage. "Remember that. No matter what you hear or what you see, it's nothing compared to what we have."

Another orgasm rocks me to my core as I come around his cock, unable to control the spasms while screaming into the sheets.

"Ah, Gia," is my only warning before he stills and comes inside me, using slow, languid strokes before easing out of me. Liquid drips from my swollen pussy, leaving a trail down the inside of my thigh.

I can't move, stuck with my head still pressed into the mattress. Every bone and muscle deliciously aches.

No one makes me feel this way other than him.

Luke chuckles and playfully nips at an ass cheek. "Are you alive?"

"Y'huh. Sure."

My legs finally give out, but I stay on my stomach, unable to move. Luke brushes the hair from my face before kissing me tenderly.

"I love you," he says, pulling me to his side.

This wasn't some means to an end. An ache to fill. It's more than a physical need. Our connection is almost spiritual. No matter what happens in our life, we know we're there for one another.

"I love you, too."

And nothing and no one will ever tear us apart. We're in this for the long haul.

CHAPTER
Fourteen

Gia

I wake up and stretch across the enormous fluffy bed, feeling every muscle fight against the strain. Last night, sleep wasn't an option. I only hope Luke doesn't have anything big planned because he will be dragging ass all day. Unless he has a few espresso shots, then he might look halfway normal.

This time, there's no pain when I see the dimple still in his pillow. I pluck it from its spot, burying my head in it and inhaling Luke's scent still clinging to the linen. I wish I could bottle this smell and take it everywhere with me. Lingering cologne, whatever shampoo he uses, a little bit of sweat and some sex and voila... instant aphrodisiac.

A note crinkles under the pillow and a slow smile forms as I lean against the headboard, still clinging to the makeshift Luke replacement.

Angel,

My staff is at your disposal this morning. Anything you need, just pick up the phone and let them know. I've taken the liberty of giving you a section in my closet where you'll find several outfits to choose from. Feel free to bring more items over to completely fill the space as needed.

You are a goddess among mortals. I will have a more pleasant day as I relive last night again and again in my head.

Yours forever and always,

Luke

Be still my heart. Obviously he knows me well enough to leave this under his pillow rather than on top.

I'm not sure he could be more romantic if he tried.

A knock at the door pulls me from my thoughts. My first instinct is to cling to the covers and not answer it. But it couldn't be his mother. She knows he's out and wouldn't come wandering into his place, let alone knock if she knew he wasn't here.

Instead, I grab Luke's shirt from the floor, thankful it comes down to my mid-thigh, and pad my way to the door. A middle-aged woman in uniform holds a tray with various plates covered in silver domes.

"Miss Hartley?"

"Yes?"

I step aside as she walks into the room, placing the tray down on the table. "His Highness ordered a breakfast platter for you this morning." I glance at the tray and fidget with the hem of the shirt. "Is there anything else you require?"

Not that she can bring for me. "Uh, no thank you. This is plenty."

"Very good, Miss. Please let us know if anything changes." She bows slightly and leaves me to my thoughts.

Correction: he can be more romantic.

I lift the first dome off the tray and my stomach growls with anticipation from the delicious aromas and assorted breakfast items. Waffles with strawberries, scrambled eggs loaded with cheese and bacon, breakfast potatoes, and three sausage links. Under the next dome is an array of various pastries, ranging from a simple blueberry scone to a chocolate croissant. Dome three contains a steaming mug of coffee and a small glass of orange juice.

I lift the mug first, humming in delight. They made it just how I like it: pale, creamy, and filled with vanilla flavor. Sitting down, I start working on the food, not realizing how much of an appetite I'd acquired after the excursions of last night.

When I can't fit anything else in my stomach, I go back to the bed and find the burner phone I stuffed in my jeans before leaving the bar last night.

Me: Have I told you how amazing and lovable you are?

I don't bother waiting for a reply. Instead, the gigantic shower with the unlimited hot water supply in his bathroom is calling my name.

The automatic lights flick on as I walk into the closet with the towel wrapped around myself. Holy shit. When he said he gave me a section, I was expecting four hangers, maybe a top drawer of some dresser. Not *half his closet*. I don't think I own enough clothes to fill this space, even if I combine what I have back home and what I have here. Not that I'd need to. He practically filled it for me. Dresses, shirts, jeans, sweaters, jackets… you name it, it's here, almost like my own mini department store. I don't know whether to kiss him or kick him.

Not surprising that everything fits perfectly, like the time he bought clothes for me in Chicago. I don't know how he does it and frankly, I don't want to. It'd take some of the mystery away from him. Or irritate me on how perfect he is.

Definitely one of those two.

After picking out a pair of jeans and a nicer top, I find the burner phone on the bed, sending little reminder beeps on an unread message.

Luke: Only because of you.

Luke: Are you there angel?

Luke: Angel???

Shit. I don't want him thinking someone found me.

Me: Don't worry, I was just enjoying your human-sized shower.

I hardly need to wait for his reply.

Luke: Please don't tell me when you're naked with water running down your body, caressing you in places I can't touch at the moment.

Me: So I shouldn't let you know how many times I lathered myself up and down, using your soap so I can smell like you?

Luke: If you don't stop, I'm going to be required to give an explanation to the press regarding my massive hard-on and I'd rather not do that.

I laugh and bite my lip.

Me: Okay, I'll behave. Just know that I love you and thank you for everything this morning. It was perfect.

Luke: Anything for you. Always and forever. X

I slide the phone into my back pocket. How lucky am I to have scored such an amazing boyfriend?

But I can't hide out here forever. One, I have work again tonight. And two, I refuse to be a kept woman.

Another knock at the door startles me, but I brush it off and find two of my favorite people.

"Amelia? Kendra? What are you doing here?"

The girls rush inside after giving me a hug. "We're under orders to take you away for the afternoon."

Like I have to ask whose.

"And what exactly are we going to do?"

Kendra smiles and hooks her arm through mine. "Help fill your section of the closet."

I scoff and practically drag them inside the massive space. "What exactly do I need to fill? He has everything here for me already."

Amelia shrugs. "We're just the messengers."

Definitely going to kick him later.

With the girls here, my escape plan was easy. The town car they rented has tinted back windows, shielding us from any unwanted eyes. Up until this moment, I hadn't really thought about how I was going to leave without drawing any attention. Luke really did think of everything. I could even get used to this sort of arrangement.

After the fourth store, I'm in dire need of a break. Luckily we were able to have all our purchases delivered to the Whittaker Estate so we didn't have to haul them around. Not sure how mine will get to Luke's place, but I know he has his ways.

A large crowd gathers at a local park as we pass by. Photographers, reporters, and TV news cameras flood the area. The excited voices of children ring above everything else.

"What's going on over there?" I ask.

Kendra shrugs. "Not sure. Should we find out?"

"Let's," says Amelia, steering us in that direction.

We manage to weave our way through the crowd, filled with families of all backgrounds and sizes. The press has taken residence at the base of a makeshift stage, set up with a microphone and ribbon meant to be cut.

"Must be some sort of dedication ceremony," I say.

Just then, excited cheers erupt from the crowd as Luke takes the stage. With Kiera's hand in his. My heart skips a few beats, turning erratic as I can't stop staring at their connection.

I look over to Kendra, who notices the same thing. Her lips move, but no sound comes out. I'm drawn back to the scene in front of me. Luke, dressed in an exquisite business suit and Kiera, elegant in a knee-length floral dress and coordinating hat.

I try to focus to stop the panic from taking over, but it's useless.

It's not real. It's all a show. It's not real.

My new mantra seems to help as background noises filter in slowly. Luke's voice rises above the rest.

"On behalf of the royal family, I'm honored to dedicate this new park to all of the families in our great capital city. Our hope is this will be a place of laughter and caring, where anyone can go no matter their station or financial status. Behind me, the recreational center will encourage more physical exercise and social skills through various sports and free programs. My foundation helped to form this center, with the help of local authorities and groups, to make sure everyone has a chance to follow their passions and grow together as a community." A round of applause sounds as he takes a scheduled pause. "This is something I'm proud of, bringing families together from all walks of life, closing the gap so everyone has the same opportunities." He pointedly looks over to a smiling Kiera. "One day, I hope to bring my own children here."

Dagger. Nail. Coffin.

No amount of chanting my mantra will take that sting away. Amelia and Kendra instantly wrap their arms around me, probably seeing the panic on my face.

"Come on, let's get out of here." We walk back to the town car and drive away, though I don't notice anything as it passes by in a blur.

"What else should we do?" Kendra asks.

I continue staring out the window. "I just want to go home."

"No, that's a horrible idea," Amelia says. "Being alone with your thoughts? You know he was just playing the game."

My brain understands that, but my heart is struggling. Staging events and holding hands is one thing. Looking at her and implying you'll have kids together is completely different.

"Please take me home."

They don't argue anymore and within minutes we're pulling up to my building at the back entrance. Both women file out behind me, each engulfing me with a bone-crushing hug. "We'll see you later, okay?"

I nod and half-heartedly return the embrace before making my way up the stairs.

And to think, today started off so well. I knew I wasn't lucky enough to get through this day unscathed. I lock the door behind me and fall face-first into my bed. This is going to be a long night.

Once again, the place is packed from wall to wall with customers, leaving hardly any room to move. Matt and I race behind the bar, trying to fill everyone's drink orders as quickly as possible.

"What's going on tonight?" I yell over the music and conversations.

"Don't know," he says. "Maybe it's a full moon?"

Which would explain my day perfectly.

The nice thing about busy nights is time moves so quickly.

Between pouring beers and introducing people to my kinds of drinks—which in turn makes everyone want one—I hardly notice when the crew shows up. Kendra stands on her tiptoes, waving a hand above the crowd. I wave back with a chuckle and finish muddling an old-fashioned.

Bryce bellies up to the bar, waiting patiently until there's a break in the action.

"Hey, gorgeous," he says.

I roll my eyes. "What did I tell you yesterday about your flirting attempts?"

He laughs and shakes his head. "I can do whatever I want."

"Uh huh. What does Amelia and Kendra want?" I don't bother asking about the guys. They're creatures of habit and order the same thing every time.

"They said something fruity and strong."

Helpful.

"Okay, I'll bring it over."

Now the question is, do I go basic or live on the edge? Ultimately, I decide on middle of the road with a French Martini, placing them on the tray with the three mugs of beer. The crowd parts, allowing me to easily reach their table without spilling a drop. Will wonders never cease.

"Hey guys," I say, distributing the drinks to everyone.

"How are you feeling?" Amelia asks, concern lacing her voice.

"Fine," I say shortly. "I'd rather not think about it."

She nods and takes a sip of her drink. "Oh my heavens. Gia, you've outdone yourself."

"Thank you." The door opens again with another group of guys pushing their way in. "I'd love to stay and chat, but something tells me it's going to be one of those nights."

"Go be awesome," Reid says, waving me away. I give them a sympathetic smile and join Matt again, trying to get ahead of the curve.

Finally, after another hour or so, things start to die down. The crowd has thinned a little, leaving us a little breathing room.

"Christ, that was crazy. It's been a while since we've had a night like this."

The cool water feels good as it slides down my throat. "Yeah, but it's fun." Busy keeps my brain turned off from the events I witnessed earlier.

After cleaning up a few empty glasses from abandoned tables, I check on my friends, noticing two new people among the ranks.

Wonderful. Showtime again.

"How are we doing over here?" My voice is overly chipper as I plaster a fake smile on my face.

Luke frowns, his eyes looking me over from head to toe. "I'll have an ale, please."

I avoid his eyes, trying to save my heart from any ache. However, I don't miss Kiera's arm draped over his as they sit next to each other.

"I'll have what those two are having." Her singsong voice irritates me mildly, but I nod and head back to the bar with my task.

Matt greets me with a sympathetic smile as I pour Luke's beer. "Are you okay?"

Giving him the same fake smile, I move onto the French Martini for Luke's "girlfriend". "Of course. Why wouldn't I be?"

I'm not fooling anyone. Matt and I have only been friends for a short time, but he's been a bartender for a lot longer and can spot bullshit when it's dealt. To my benefit, he doesn't call me out on it and lets me go about my business.

The closer I get to the table, the more I feel a certain set of eyes on me. Concerning eyes. But I can't think about them right now. Instead, I slide up my armor and pretend nothing's wrong.

"Here you go." It wasn't my intention to mock Kiera's singsong voice. It just happened. She either didn't make the connection or she chose not to acknowledge it.

Kendra tilts her head. "Are you okay?"

Shit, I'm fucking this up. "Yeah, of course." Before she has a chance to dissect this more, I head back to the bar to get away from the situation.

At least if Simon shows up, he'll see I'm not happy about their presence. Maybe I can chalk this up to playing the part?

Even though I'm far enough away from the group, I still can see everything going on. Each laugh and motion draw my attention. Kiera hanging on Luke's every word. Kiera clinging to his arm like a life preserver. Kiera telling jokes. Kiera smiling. Kiera this. Kiera that.

What's the definition of insanity again?

I'm about to let it drop when I look up and see her lips pressed against his. Not passionately, but quick. Almost matronly.

I can't.

Red tinges my vision as I toss the rag into the sink.

"Matt, I'll be right back. I need to check on something."

He doesn't question my sudden mood change, probably seeing the reason himself. "Take your time. I'll be okay for a while."

Without another look, I walk to the office—needing to get away from the situation—and sit on the edge of the desk, bending at the waist while resting my head in my hands.

The door clicks shut and I whip my head up to see Luke standing before me, still in his dress slacks but with a more casual shirt.

"Gia." Pain laces his voice, knowing I saw what happened out there. "I swear—"

Before he has a chance to finish his sentence, I attack his mouth, leaving no room to mistake my desperation and need. I walk him back until he bumps into the door, giving me access to turn the lock. The last thing we need is a witness to what we're about to do.

With deft fingers, I make quick work of his belt and pants, satisfied as they drop to the floor. I break the kiss, staring directly into his eyes as I sink down, keeping my hands on his chest, feeling every muscle contract on the way down.

"Angel." It's a warning. I know he thinks I don't need to do this, but it's not for me or him. It's for us.

I drag his boxer briefs down his legs, freeing the beast inside. My mouth waters as I take him in my hands, loving the silky feel of him against my palms. Hard yet soft, like steel wrapped in velvet. Luke groans as I work his shaft slowly, still keeping my gaze. I lean forward and flick my tongue against the sensitive head, satisfied as he jerks and twitches in my hand.

Like last night, I'm not into foreplay right now. Without another second to lose, I wrap my lips around his length, working my way down his shaft, sucking and licking until I hit the base, my nose squished against his skin.

"Fuck, Gia." I'm thankful for my lack of gag reflex as I breathe through my nose, taking my time to slide back and forth against his cock.

Nothing makes a woman feel more powerful than having her man come apart in the palm of her hands. Literally.

I alternate between slow and hard licks, light suction and gliding across his skin while teasing his sensitive head. Each moan spurs me on, fueling my need and desire to show how much I need him.

The first twitch in my mouth indicates he's not going to last much longer.

We never break eye contact as I bob my head faster, twisting and twirling, knowing how much it drives him mad. He swells even more; his salty taste dances across my tongue.

"I can't... Gia..."

But I won't let him get off that easy. Pun intended.

Saliva clings to my lips as I pull away, breathing hard while running my hands up and down his thighs before gripping his shaft again. His hips keep time with my ministrations, fueling me forward to wrap my lips around his cock again, taking no prisoners.

Luke tangles a hand in my hair, gripping tight, trying to take back some control, but it's no use. I'm a woman on a mission.

"Give it to me," I say, licking him from the base all the way to the tip. "Give me what I want."

"And what's that, angel?" He knows damn well but wants to hear me beg anyway.

A devilish smirk crosses my lips as I use the tip of my tongue to run along the grooves of his head, teasing the crown until his eyes practically roll backward.

"All of you."

The grip he has on my hair tightens when I fully take him to the back of my throat. His control wanes, his movements jerkier than each one before.

"Ah, Gia," is my only warning before he swells inside my mouth and I taste the first spurts of cum that shoot out of him. I take him farther to the back of my throat, swallowing around his shaft and everything he has to give.

Wetness coats my cheeks as I pull away, feeling satisfied in the knowledge that I'm the one who can bring him to his knees. I'm the one who can do this.

I don't care if my makeup is ruined or my hair is a mess. We both needed this.

Luke pulls me off the floor, gripping the sides of my face and crashing his lips onto mine, delving his tongue into my mouth to taste himself.

"Please, angel, tell me you weren't jealous."

I match his pose and return the favor. "I wanted to remind you of who you belong to."

He smiles, brushing away the hair from my face and running a thumb under the probable black smudges showing under my eyes. "It's always you."

"Good. Remember that." I kiss him again, this time softer, gentler. "Oh and tell Kiera that kissing is off-limits."

"I will." We adjust our clothing until we're both decent. "We should probably head back out there."

I nod. "You go first. I need to check my makeup and probably fix my hair."

He growls slightly, sending another pulse to my already aching pussy. "You've never looked sexier than you do in this moment."

"Barbarian." He takes my mouth again in another heated kiss and it kills me to push him away as I unlock the door. "At least your hair already looked like you had sex today."

"And I remember it vividly." Luke palms a breast and I slap his hand away before anything else can happen. This wasn't about my pleasure. This was all for him.

"Go!" I practically push him out of the office door. He pauses in the doorway, stealing another kiss before turning down the hall and back to the main floor.

I blow out a quick breath and check my reflection in the mirror. Hair a tangled mess, mascara running, lips swollen and red. Nothing that can't be fixed.

Once I'm put back together—thanks to the pale pink lip gloss I always keep in my apron—I head back to the bar and re-join Matt, who's sporting a shit-eating grin.

"Enjoy your break?"

Red tinges my cheeks as I try to focus on cleaning the counters. "Very much." God, I hope we weren't too loud. I look up and see several of our friends look my way, sporting similar smirks as Matt. Fuckers.

It doesn't matter. Even though this plan is killing me slowly, I know in the end that Luke and I will be together.

CHAPTER
Fifteen

Gia

I gaze at the snow-covered peaks as we drive down the winding road, the curves almost lulling me to sleep. Our little ski holiday requires two rented SUVs to haul everyone and our things. Who knew you needed so much stuff for a week-long vacation?

Thanks to Luke and his generous shopping spree, I have more than enough sweaters and winter wear to last more than our little getaway allows. My only issue was limiting my packing to one bag. Granted, the bag was large enough to fit a small person inside it, but that was beside the point.

We crest a hill and my jaw drops to the floor. An enormous lodge comes into view, something straight out of a movie. Rustic with log features and old-world European charm. You can see the ski hill and lifts behind it—which, not going to lie, is a little intimidating. I can count on one hand how many times I've been skiing. Somehow I doubt the small hills at a Wisconsin vacation resort will compare to these mammoth slopes.

"Damn," I mutter as Connor parks in the valet line.

The cold, bitter wind feels good against my face as I step out of the car. Almost feels like home. It's crazy to think I've missed something so annoying.

"You like?" Kendra slides up next to me, slinging her arm around my shoulders.

"I think I'm in love." Not with the whole skiing idea, but lounging around a fireplace, sipping drinks, and laughing with friends? Count me in.

We walk into the lobby and I can't seem to close my mouth. I didn't know rustic could be high-end as well. Assorted animal antlers tastefully decorate the walls. Not like some hunting shack where you can feel the eyes following your every movement. They've even used them as a grand chandelier. Two fireplaces—one on each side—roar with orange flames and embers. Several leather couches and chairs surround the hearth, all occupied by guests enjoying the warmth while laughing.

"We'll go check us in," Amelia says, dragging her husband to the front desk.

The sheer size of this place is a wonder all on its own.

"What does everyone want to do first?" Kendra asks.

Reid shrugs. "I'm game for anything."

"Hit the slopes?" Bryce shrugs.

I'm still a little too awestruck to let my brain fully function. But I know enough that I'd rather not break my leg right away. "How about we unpack and relax?"

They look at me like I'm crazy. "And give up this perfect day?" Kendra gasps.

Ooookay. Looks like I'll be tackling the bunny hill right away. "You know that I don't ski, right?"

"Skiing is easy," Reid says. "Just bend your knees and go."

Yeah, sure. Okay. "It's not the mechanics of it, more like a fear of falling off the lift or down the side of a cliff." Not to mention the last time I skied, I was practically bent in half with my back *and* skis on the ground at the same time. I'm surprised I didn't blow out a knee. My sister and friends got a good laugh out of it as I rounded the corner looking like an idiot.

"Please. That hardly ever happens," Bryce says, shaking his head.

"Hardly isn't never." Which implies I'm not completely off base with my fears.

I'm about to go into a full-blown panic when Amelia and Connor come back with the room keys.

"Bryce and Reid," Connor says, handing them their little folder. "Kendra." Wait, what? "And Gia."

"Hold up. Why aren't we staying together?" I wave a finger between me and Kendra. "Those two are sharing a room."

"Because there's—" Connor starts but Amelia slaps a hand over his mouth.

"We just thought you'd like the quiet and relaxation with all the stress you've been under lately. In fact, we preordered a massage for you once you arrive upstairs." She smiles sweetly. Almost *too* sweetly. "Consider this a stress-free zone for the next seven days."

Stress-free? Do I even know what that is? But I'm not about to pass up a free massage.

"You didn't have to do that for me."

Reid smirks. "Don't worry. We didn't."

Luke. Of course. He's even taking care of me when he's away on business. The last few weeks have been better. We meet up after I'm done closing and sneak off to his place or when time is pressed, just stay at mine. The empty spot next to me in the morning isn't so bad anymore. Not when he leaves behind a shirt or note or something else to let me know he's thinking of me. I've even gotten better at ignoring the papers, avoiding newsstands whenever possible so I'm not tempted to see the garbage displayed on the front page. Whatever we're doing must be working because Simon hasn't shown his face in the bar the last few days. Maybe Marguerite has finally called off the dogs.

"Okay, let's get settled and meet back here for dinner. That way everyone can hit the slopes or just relax if they want," Connor says, pulling Amelia into his arms. I think we all know what they'll be doing.

Honeymooners.

Everyone gets off on the same floor... except me. My room is on the top floor for whatever reason. I'm guessing another surprise left for me by a certain someone. I'm not used to having all these lavish gifts bestowed upon me. I'm a simple girl with simple tastes, which he knows. Give me a hot dog and a beer and I'm good to go.

Déjà vu hits as I walk down the hall toward the only door on this side. How big is this room? I'm only one person. When the guys stayed in Chicago, they had something similar, but they were four people. Luke must be out of his mind.

The door swings open and I drop everything in my hands, lifting them to cover my mouth so I don't scream.

Roses. So many roses.

Red, yellow, white, peach... every color imaginable.

Long stems in the vases. Petals on the floor.

I move my things out of the way to lock myself into this romantic wonderland. I can't even begin to imagine how he managed this, though I'm sure a prince would be able to do just about anything he wanted. I lean down to sniff one of the bouquets. The scent is so intoxicating.

The room is as big as I anticipated. Large, eat-in kitchen open to a lavish living room, complete with a huge TV set above a fireplace. A separate dining area with seats for eight, which could come in handy if we all want to hang out later.

There is a door on each side of the room, but only one has petals leading to it. I head to the other door and peek inside, seeing a perfectly put together bedroom, complete with its own en suite bathroom. Good Lord. If this is just the spare room, I can't imagine what the master will look like.

I turn on my heels and follow the path led before me, swinging the door open for yet another surprise.

And this one takes the cake.

Luke. Naked, waiting for me on the bed, lying on his side, with his head propped up in one hand and holding a vase of flowers to cover his manhood in the other.

"Oh, is this a new hotel service? I didn't know I could expect a sexy royal prince in my bed."

He smirks, setting the vase down on the bedside table. "*Our* bed."

"What?"

Slowly, he stands and stalks toward me. It's hard not to stare as his cock stands at half-mast. I lick my lips without thinking before making eye contact with him only inches away.

"See something you like?" He quirks a brow and I can feel the heat rise up my cheeks. Luke brushes the back of his hand against my face, bending down quickly to place a chaste kiss upon my lips. "It so happens that my business is in the city nearby, so this is our room for the week."

That sneaky, conniving little… I'll have to thank Kendra later for putting this all together. One whole week of not hiding in the shadows, of waking up next to him, making love in the middle of the night for no reason other than we need each other.

"Mmm, I like the sound of that." I stand on my tiptoes and sling my arms around his neck, pulling him in for a proper kiss. He licks my bottom lip and I eagerly open, waiting for his tongue to possess every inch of my mouth. "This will be heaven," I say against his lips.

Luke takes a small step back. Guilt wracks his eyes. "One small hitch."

Figures we'd never get off that easy. "What's that?"

He bites his lower lip. "Kiera's here as well."

"Oh," I say, dragging my fingers across his toned abs. "Is that all?"

His eyes dilate and darken, staying perfectly still while I continue to explore the vast expanse of skin before me. "I thought you'd be more upset."

Trailing my fingers lower, I take a step closer. "Does she get all your attention after the events are done?"

Luke hisses as I brush against his length, now completely ready to go. "No."

"Then I don't care," I say, wrapping a hand around and giving him a few good pumps.

"Angel." He crashes his lips onto mine, need and want mixing together, stripping me out of my clothes until everything is on the floor. Somehow he manages to guide me onto the bed, flipping me over so I'm on my stomach.

"Keep your eyes closed."

I can hardly wait to see what he has in store as I follow his directions. Something wet and slightly cold hits the middle of my back, pooling along the divot of my spine. Luke spreads the substance around, kneading every muscle and finding every knot along the way.

"Oooohhhh goooodddddd," I moan indecently, pulling a laugh from Luke.

"If you keep making sounds like that, you'll never get through this massage."

Hmm, keep moaning and get some dick or be quiet and have him oil me up, touching every inch of my body with his hands.

These are tough decisions.

But I stay quiet—or as quiet as I can be—while Luke continues to relieve the stress I've been carrying. I always knew he had magic fingers, but damn. A girl could get used to this.

"Okay, turn over." His voice turns husky, gritty, filled with need. My favorite voice.

I do as requested and I'm rewarded with a front row seat to his straining cock. Luke takes a moment to appreciate my body, scanning every inch and setting it on fire with his gaze. With oil-slicked hands, he palms my breasts, giving them rapt attention as I try to suppress the moan begging to be released.

That's not the only thing begging for release.

With Luke straddling my hips, I'm locked in place. He reaches for my arms, dragging them above my head, massaging the muscles on his way back down. The moment he makes contact with my breasts again, I arch my back off the bed, this time not caring about what sounds I make.

"Luke, please."

He leans forward and presses his lips against mine, teasingly slow. "Would you like a happy ending?"

His right hand leaves my chest, trailing down my stomach—which flutters under his touch—until he finds his destination between my legs.

"Ah! Yes!"

The world tilts on its axis as his lips follow the same path as his hand, leaving me aching and crying out his name over and over.

Once we're showered up and ready to join society again, Luke and I walk hand in hand to the lobby where are friends are waiting near one of the fireplaces. Something we'd never be allowed to do normally, but Luke assured me this is the one place we're safe to be ourselves. Apparently, this lodge is a well-known, highly secure hideaway to celebrities and royals alike, giving them freedom away from scrutinizing eyes and shameless photographers. Protected against the threats of the outside world. A place to truly be yourself.

"Look who decided to join," Reid says with a smirk. "Bryce, you owe me money."

"Damn," he says, folding a bill and passing it to a smug Reid. "I thought I had a solid bet."

I laugh and look between the two of them. "Sorry, but we came here to have fun with the rest of you too."

Luke kisses my forehead and holds me close to his chest. "So where do we have dinner reservations?"

Kendra smiles and stands. "At the in-house restaurant. Figured this would be easier than driving all the way into town."

Good point.

Kiera stands and comes up to us. "Thank you for being so good about everything. I can't imagine how you must feel. I'd be devastated if I had to watch the person I love pretend to be with someone else."

It's hard to feel any ill will toward her. She's done nothing wrong. No, all the blame lies solely on one person.

"Hopefully it won't be much longer."

She nods and smiles brightly. "Honestly, I'm envious of you," she whispers. "Of what you both have. One day I hope to find a little of that magic with someone."

Kiera really is a sweet girl. I wiggle away from Luke's hold and engulf her in a hug. "You will. I'm sure of it."

We sit around the table tucked away in a private room in the upscale restaurant, sharing stories and laughing until we're practically in tears. It's exactly the type of getaway we've been craving.

After dinner, everyone heads to our room since it has the most space and we order several bottles of wine and whiskey to enjoy around the large fireplace.

"I can't believe it's only the two of you staying here," Kendra says, pouring another glass of wine. She stumbles back to her spot on the couch, sitting *just* a bit closer to Reid each time. I smile when she looks my way; cheeks rosy from both the wine and the man sitting next to her. Reid is a fool if he doesn't see how much she likes him now.

"It is a lot of space for us, but it's also the best. And Gia deserves the best," Luke says, resting his arm across my shoulders. I snuggle into his side and fight off the urge to sleep. I'm warm, comfortable, and the alcohol is flowing through me like water.

Hopefully Luke doesn't suffer from whiskey dick. Although the few times we've been out drinking, it seems to have the opposite effect. Maybe I should get my sleep in now because there's a chance I won't get any later.

Bryce starts another horror story from one of his clients last week, leaving us all in stitches from the absurdity.

Luke kisses my head again and I sigh. We definitely needed this vacation together.

Somehow Kendra and Amelia talked me into getting off the bunny hill and onto one of the actual slopes. Sure, it's only a level one beginner slope, but I'm not about to break my neck anytime soon. Unfortunately, Luke will be working during the day all week, so he's missing all the fun. He did, however, request a video of me skiing, which all the guys volunteered to take. Assholes.

When not on the slopes, we're either in the chalet or leaving the guys to go shopping in town, except for Kiera who joins Luke for a few functions to keep up the rouse.

By midweek, we've become so comfortable with everything, it's going to be hard to go back to normal, hiding our relationship rather than present it to the world with no cares or consequences.

On a rare afternoon off, Luke drags me to a cross-country ski trail, where skiing isn't all we do. We veer off course and make out in a small wooded area, pressing each other against the trees, falling into snowdrifts, and acting like two teenagers sneaking out of the house, leading into a snowball fight—which of course I won.

Sitting around the fireplace again in our room, the eight of us decide to order takeout and play games. Charades is up first, leaving us all in stitches as Bryce attempts to act out *The Sound of Music* and fails miserably.

"Please don't quit your day job to go into acting," I say between peals of laughter. Bryce sticks out his tongue before reclaiming his seat next to Kiera and draining the contents of his glass.

"It's not my fault you all suck."

We keep laughing and giving each other a hard time until the alcohol runs out, each of our cheeks rosy and balance slightly off.

"We should probably get to bed," Connor says, running his hands up and down Amelia's sides as he stands behind her.

Judging by all our levels of intoxication, might not be a bad idea. We only have two more days left and no one wants to spend one hungover.

After saying our goodbyes, Luke locks the door, turning to me with predatory eyes. "Finally." I squeal and run back to the bedroom with Luke hot on my heels. Once he catches me, he attacks my mouth with passion and tosses me on the bed.

Thank God whiskey has the opposite effect.

By morning, most everyone is down in the restaurant, eating everything greasy we can find on the menu. Luke, of course, is not here, attending the last meeting of the week. Part of me understands, yet the larger part wishes he was here. Kiera gives a sympathetic smile and pulls out the chair next to me.

"It's hard when his life isn't his own."

I nod. "I know. It's just... I've never dated someone with such a demanding career. I'm used to simple and easy. Fun. Then add in all this crap with his mom and I'm beside myself on what to do."

She places a hand on my forearm. "It'll get easier. I think it's difficult now because you need to hide. When it comes out, you'll feel much better."

Assuming his mother doesn't tank us first.

I plaster on a smile, trying to believe she's right. "I'm sure I will." There's no conviction in my statement and thankfully she doesn't call me on it.

"Has anyone seen Kendra?" Amelia asks. "It's odd she isn't down here yet."

Come to think of it, it is strange. She's not one to miss a meal.

"She didn't make it back to the room last night," Kiera says with a shrug.

Huh. "And where's Reid?"

"No idea. I was dead to the world once I hit the mattress. Reid's door was still shut when I left the suite," Bryce adds.

Speak of the devils. Both Reid and Kendra walk into the restaurant looking slightly guilty and a little hungover, each sporting sunglasses to either counteract the intrusion of light or hide their eyes from the rest of us.

Curious.

They take the two remaining chairs, coincidentally next to each other. Reid goes to pull out her chair at the same time Kendra does, leaving them with an awkward exchange.

Amelia and I raise a brow and exchange a suspicious glance.

"What's good today?" Kendra says, hiding behind the menu. Reid stays quiet, avoiding any eye contact from the five of us.

"I hear the stuffed French toast is excellent."

Kendra's cheeks turn pink. "I think I'll just have some eggs and bacon."

"Me too," says Reid, setting his menu down.

Do we bring up the elephant in the room or wait it out? Surely I can't be the only one curious about this situation. I don't want to thrust them into the spotlight if they don't want to be there. I know how it feels and I wouldn't wish that on anyone.

By nightfall, we're all incredibly exhausted after another round on the slopes. My body is practically a popsicle after falling on every run I went on. Kendra tried to convince me to come out one last time, but my toes feel like sausages and I can barely move. Instead, a swim in the tub with candles and a bath bomb are calling my name.

The warm vanilla and lavender scents instantly ease the

tension as I close my eyes and practically fall asleep in the warm oasis. I barely hear the bathroom door open and click shut. I smile as Luke climbs in, wrapping his arms around my waist and pulling me into his chest with my head resting against his shoulder.

"Here you are," he says, kissing my neck. "I thought maybe you'd be out with the others."

I hum my pleasure and wrap my arms around his, keeping us close. "Too cold outside. This was a better idea."

Luke trails his hands up and down my sides. "I agree." He skims the side of my breasts, stirring a need from deep within.

Water sloshes over the side of the tub as I turn around to straddle his lap, running my hands through his hair before pressing our lips and bodies together.

"I love you," I say, lifting up and slowly sinking down on top of him.

Luke groans and deepens the kiss, gripping my hips while controlling the tempo. Slow and steady, reverent and sensual. Loving me in a way only he knows how.

"I love you too, angel."

CHAPTER
Sixteen

Gia

Not going to lie, leaving our safe bubble at the ski lodge was tough. Being open and free, not having to look over my shoulder every waking second was a beautiful respite. But now in the cold grip of reality, we're back to the land of make-believe.

Guess I'm a little salty over the whole situation.

I just want everything to be over and done. Being with Luke is all I need. Having the future I never planned on. But if his mother doesn't approve, I can't see a way around this.

Kendra pulls into the drive at her parents' house, skyrocketing my nerves up another notch. I haven't seen or spoken to Miriam or Thomas since the incident at the gala. With their close relationship to the royal family, I'm not sure how warm of a reception I'll receive. There's a good chance I'll get kicked out on my ass the moment I step foot in the door. They probably burned all the things I left behind in my room. Not that I'd blame them.

"It'll be okay, I promise." Kendra's reassuring words don't do anything to calm my nerves or stop me from wringing my hands in my lap.

"What if they hate me?"

"They don't hate you."

"You don't know that," I say, chewing on my thumbnail. "They could be telling you one thing, trying to lure me in only to throw down a blow once I step foot inside."

Kendra shuts the car off and turns to me with a frown. "You watch too many suspense movies."

Not wrong. My imagination goes into overdrive when I'm nervous. When I'm really scared, I can almost bet on being a walking Murphy's Law.

I rub my sweaty hands on my jeans and climb out of the car, along with Kendra. Blowing out a quick breath, I chew on my bottom lip as a familiar face opens the door.

"Ms. Hartley, so good to see you," George says with a bright smile.

A good start, I guess.

Kendra leads the way through the massive house straight to the living room where both her parents are reading books in their fancy wingback chairs.

"Hi Mum, Dad."

They both look up, smiling brightly at their daughter. Almost in slow motion, their gazes swing my way, the smiles freezing on their faces.

Crap.

Miriam abandons her book and walks our way. Each step raises my heart rate as I fight back the panic bubbling to the surface.

"Gia, I'm so glad you're okay." She engulfs me in a

bone-crushing hug, barely giving me time to adjust my arms from being pinned to my sides.

Not the reaction I was expecting.

"Mrs. Whittaker, I—"

"Shh," she says, hugging me tighter. "Don't you dare apologize. You've done nothing wrong. The way those newspapers have been dragging your name through the mud is shameful."

Tears well in my eyes as I finally wrap my arms around this woman who treats me like one of her own. "It's been hard, and I try to avoid them whenever possible."

"I can only imagine. Here, come sit." She leads me to the plush couch, practically pushing me down. Kendra sits next to me with an "I told you so" smirk.

Miriam reclaims her seat and leans forward. "What have you been up to? Where are you staying? You know you can always come back to your old room upstairs."

I tuck some hair behind my ears and chew on my bottom lip. "Oh, thank you, but it won't be necessary. I actually have a cute apartment in town, above the bar I work at."

"That's wonderful. I know how much you enjoyed your job back home. Is this one similar?"

I nod. "Very. And Matt's been wonderful, working with me while all this is going on. Luckily, nothing major has come up."

Miriam raises a brow. "Implying something else has?"

Shit. I pick at my nails and keep my eyes diverted from hers. "Well, it appears I have a follower."

"Like a stalker?" Thomas chimes in.

"No, nothing like that," I say, appreciating the Papa Bear coming out.

Kendra turns and scoffs. "Well, he's sort of like a stalker." She turns to her mother and frowns. "It's Simon."

A look passes between Thomas and Miriam before they both nod. "I see." For a moment, I think they'll elaborate, giving away more information. But no. Silence.

"It's not a big deal. He comes in, sits at a table, and watches everything."

Again, Miriam says nothing, schooling her face into an unreadable mask. "Outside of the one person, how have the customers been to you?"

And just like that, Simon is forgotten as we fall into easy conversation, laughing and joking, catching up on everything that's happened.

"Actually, there are a few things I'd like to get from upstairs. Would that be okay?"

Miriam smiles and nods. "Of course. Like I said, you're more than welcome to stay here whenever you like."

Hmm, maybe Luke and I could use this as a secret getaway retreat, though it'd feel a little like we're having sex while a parent is home. I'd hate for Thomas and Miriam to think I'm using their place for booty calls.

"Luke is invited too," she adds with a wink.

The woman has amazing psychic powers.

"How did you know we're still together?"

Miriam takes my hand. "Dear, I've known him since he was a young boy. He's practically one of my own. Which is why I knew the rumors going on about you were false. The way you two look at each other, it's easy to see how in love you are."

I blush and look down. "Really?"

She cups my cheek and smiles. "Absolutely. Don't worry, everything will blow over and be fine."

I can only hope so.

Kendra turns and places a hand on my shoulder. "Gia, why don't you head upstairs. I'll meet you there."

The long corridors don't seem quite as scary and beyond my belief, I don't manage to get lost on the way to my old room. A wave of sadness hits me as I open the door, seeing everything still exactly as I left it. The closet still has all of the clothes Kendra bought for me; the bathroom counter still littered with the high-end makeup I barely touched. I stare at the plush king-size bed, my back aching for relief instantly. I've been trying to save up for a new bed for the apartment, but I haven't had time to go shopping yet.

I flop onto the bed, letting out an audible sigh as I sink down into the pillowy down comforter.

"You can always move back," Kendra says from the doorway. "It really hasn't been the same around here without you. Plus, it was kind of like having a sister around."

I prop myself up on my elbows and give a small smile. "I can't go back."

She takes a seat next to me and pats my hand. "I know. It feels like taking a step in the wrong direction."

Oh good. She understands. "Exactly. Not to mention I don't want your mom and dad involved in any way. This is my fight. Mine and Luke's. It's already bad enough there are so many others we've dragged into this charade." I hold my head in my hands. "It's getting exhausting."

Kendra lays down on the bed and pats my pillow. "Come on, get some sleep. With the suitcases under your eyes, it's a wonder you're even functioning right now."

Pink creeps up my neck. Sure, stress has played a part in my lack of sleep. But it's not the only thing. Luke hasn't helped either. Not physically, but the late-night sexcapades have been *more* than satisfying.

Time to turn the tables. "So, want to talk about what happened that night at the lodge?"

Kendra instantly flushes red and shakes her head. "What's next with the plan?" she says, trying to divert the conversation.

"Oh, no. I've given you plenty of time to come clean. It's been a week and I still haven't gotten any details. Spill it, Whittaker."

Suddenly, she sits up and stretches her arms, looking pointedly at her watch. "My goodness, look at the time. We should head back to the city so you can get ready for work."

"Smooth," I say under my breath. "I will get it out of you eventually."

"Nope," she singsongs before quickly darting out the door.

If I wasn't already interested in the details before, I'm more than intrigued now.

Reid has been really good about playing the part. Taking me out for public lunches, sitting at the bar while I'm working, giving me rides when Kendra or Bryce aren't available. It's like our friendship has gone back to normal, which means maybe I can get the information out of him since Kendra has remained a vault.

"Talked to Kendra lately?" I ask, pushing the salad around with my fork.

Reid doesn't flinch or show any sign of emotion as he bites into his sandwich. "Not since we all went out the other night."

Damn. He might be worse than Kendra.

The fork clangs against the plate as I steeple my hands under my chin. "You know, we couldn't help but notice the two of you at the lodge sporting some similar looks while coming to breakfast together."

"We weren't together," he quickly dismissed. "We just happened to get to the elevator at the same time."

"Both looking guilty?"

He finally picks his head up, still showing no emotion. "Why would we be guilty?"

"Oh, I don't know. Maybe acting on some feelings?"

Reid stares at me for a second. You can practically see the wheels turning in his mind as he formulates his response. "You must have still been hungover. Or sex-drunk with your rose-colored glasses."

There was no way I was mistaken about what I saw. Amelia saw it too. We've been trying to get it out of both of them and they adamantly deny everything.

But I don't want things to be awkward with a constant inquiry. Maybe eventually they'll tell the truth.

"I happen to like my sex-drunk love glasses," I say, taking an overly large bite with a smirk.

Reid laughs, but quickly frowns when a flash of light shines through the café window.

"Fucking photographers."

I was hoping we'd be out of the spotlight by now. Most of the headlines focus on Luke and Kiera, hardly a mention of us anymore.

The murmurs inside the café increase as people drag their phones out, aiming them at the door.

Now I see why.

Luke walks in with Kiera's arm draped over his. I quickly look to Reid, who appears just as shocked as me.

"Did you two plan this?"

He shakes his head. "No. We've been trying to avoid any daytime interactions."

Great.

The host guides them to a table near us, putting Luke directly in my line of sight. Our eyes connect and I can feel the pulse between us as a slow smile graces his lips.

I shake my head and quickly break our gaze, praying no one saw that.

Reid chews slowly, keeping his eyes on me. "Be careful. You're playing with fire."

"I know," I harshly whisper. "I'm not the one who needs the reminder."

No matter what I do, I can feel his eyes on my every move. It excites and scares me at the same time. I push my plate to the side, no longer hungry. "I'll be right back."

The chair screeches slightly as I walk toward the bathrooms in the back, needing to get away from the situation. As soon as the door closes behind me, I breathe a sigh of relief. We can't be here together. People will know how we feel. I can't pretend to be with someone else when the love of my life is sitting two tables away staring at me.

After fixing my hair and checking my makeup, I exit the room only to run into the hard chest of the one person I'm trying to avoid.

"Hmm, this seems familiar." He chuckles, firmly gripping my waist.

Images of the first time I saw him flutter into my head, repeating this exact situation when I needed a break from his magnetism.

"Luke, you shouldn't be here. What if people notice?"

He drags us into a dark corner, mildly shielding us. "No one will care." He bites his lip as I gaze up at his through my lashes. Leaning down, he captures my lips roughly, our teeth clashing at the intensity and need.

Fuck it.

I thread my fingers through his hair, gripping the strands and tugging until he moans into my mouth. A rush of desire sends a pulse straight to my core. Luke as well, pinning my hips to the wall so I can feel just how much he wants me.

A few noises sound at the end of the hall, breaking us apart. I try to gather my breath and slow my heart rate while Luke continues to run his hands up and down my sides.

"You should go first. It'll look strange if we walk out together," I say, leaning against the wall.

He adjusts himself in his pants. "I may need a few more minutes." I turn to walk away but he catches my arm, pulling my back to his chest. His warm breath beats against my ear. "Tonight." We both know what he means. With a kiss to the back of my head, he lets me go as I try to fix my appearance before walking to the main floor. I swipe at my lips, hoping they don't look like I just made out with someone in a hallway. A nagging feeling of being watched settles over me, but I brush it away.

Reid signs the slip as I take my seat, eyeing me skeptically. "Ready?"

He knows. There's no way he doesn't. I'm sure the flush of my cheeks gives me away and he had enough sense to secure our escape as soon as possible.

"Let's go."

He places a hand at the small of my back, helping me out the door.

I think Luke and I need to discuss our endgame, and soon. Otherwise we're going to lose our advantage and possibly the game.

CHAPTER
Seventeen

Luke

Buzz. *Buzz. Buzz.*

What in the…?

Blinking the sleep from my eyes, I lift my head up to see where that annoying noise is coming from. I lean over the bed and find my phone dancing across the floor.

I knit my brows together as I stare at the screen. Why is David calling me?

"Yes?"

"Sir, I'm on the way over to pick you up. You missed your morning appointment with Her Majesty."

What? No.

Wait.

Shit!

I look over at Gia's sleeping form, still curled toward me and peacefully unaware of the shitstorm about to come down.

How could we have been so careless? I haven't stayed the

night here since she first moved in and for good reason. Sneaking around in the shadows is easy. No one looks for you in the dark. But in broad daylight?

How am I going to rectify this?

"Thank you, David. I'll meet you out back in ten minutes."

I end the call and toss the phone on the bed. Looking over at Gia again, I don't have the heart to wake her. She's been through enough because of my mother. Alerting her to this possible hazard would only add more stress.

Slowly, quietly, I slink from underneath the covers, careful not to make a sound. Gia moans and shifts, stretching her hand out toward the spot I just vacated. I hate this. Hate sneaking away when all I want is to hold her in my arms all day and night.

I lean over and kiss her naked shoulder, allowing my lips to linger a second longer than necessary. I love the way her silky smooth skin feels, still smelling like sex and something inherently Gia. Each time I leave her alone, it's getting harder and harder to walk away.

I change in record time, not caring how wrinkled my clothes are. After cleaning myself up in the bathroom as best I can, I walk back to her room and chuckle. That poor pillow. She has a death grip on it, clutching it to her chest.

"I love you," I whisper before kissing her cheek.

"Love you," she mutters, still asleep.

I lock the door behind me—thankful she gave me a key—and walk straight to the waiting car. David tips his hat and opens the back door for me.

"Cutting it close, sir."

Don't I know it. "Thank you."

Once I'm in the back seat, David pulls away from Gia's building and straight into the morning traffic.

"I took the liberty of grabbing a few items for you to change into, sir."

To my left is my favorite gray suit and the emergency travel kit. Once this whole ordeal is done, David will be getting a raise.

"Thank you, David." I raise the divider so I can quickly change.

By the time I walk into the great hall, my mother is sitting in the receiving room, sipping tea while talking with someone, only I can't see who.

I pull out my phone and send a quick text to Kiera, letting her know that I stayed the night at her place, should anyone ask.

Mother looks up as I slide the phone into my jacket pocket. "Ah, Lucien. Please, join us."

The person sitting opposite them stands, bows, and leaves in the other direction. Odd.

I take the vacated seat and sit back, waving off a servant who brings over a tray with coffee.

"We missed you this morning at breakfast. Where were you?" There's an air of suspicion in her voice, sending up my defenses instantly.

I must tread lightly so I don't tip her off.

"I spent the night at Kiera's place."

She raises a brow. "Oh? Have things finally progressed to that point?"

"Yes," I say, resting my arms on the back of the couch. "We're happy together."

Her skilled mask of indifference stays firmly in place as she lifts the cup to her lips. "Good. Then we should be expecting an engagement announcement soon."

"Yes, you will." Only it won't be with Kiera.

Ever since Gia arrived in Lecara, it's the only thing I've

thought about, seeing my ring on her finger, binding us together so no one could tear us apart. Whether or not it'll be with a royal blessing has yet to be seen.

Only one person can make that decision and she's sitting right in front of me.

"Good. Nothing would make me happier than to see our two great families joined together."

Thomas enters the room again with a bow. "Your next appointment is here, Your Majesty."

"Send him in," she says, giving her tea to the servant who's cleaning up around us. I start to walk away but pause when she calls my name. "In the future, try to be more considerate of your schedule. Tardiness is unbecoming of a prince."

I grit my teeth and nod. "I'll do better in the future, Mother."

"Please do," she says with a final dismissal.

That was close.

I head back to my house to properly get ready for my day. Luckily, all my meetings are in the afternoon, so I won't be rushed.

But first...

I pick up my phone and call David.

"Sir?"

As soon as my bedroom doors shut, I undo the tie and toss it on my bed. "I need you to order a dozen roses and send Ms. Hartley lunch to her apartment this afternoon."

"The usual?"

Since David has been instructed to treat Gia the same as me, he's gotten to know her tastes, what restaurants she likes, her favorite colors. Whatever I know, he knows.

"Absolutely."

It's the least I can do after sneaking out so abruptly this morning. What woman doesn't like being surprised by random gifts from her boyfriend?

"Consider it done, sir."

I strip out of my clothes and find my way into the shower, letting the water cascade over me until all my worries disappear down the drain.

Gia and I kept a low profile the last few days after our near mistake. Mother has been overly curious about my whereabouts, inquiring about my daily activity and requesting updates whenever I have meetings. I haven't even been able to sneak away to the Boar and Bear to catch a glimpse of Gia in person. Our late-night interactions have been limited to simple good night texts.

Kiera has been supportive through all of this, which I greatly appreciate. Kendra and Bryce as well, passing along little notes while keeping me updated on her happiness. That's my main concern.

Unfortunately, my duties take me out of town for the next few days doing business for the crown. I hate these public relations tours, going out to have photo ops with dignitaries for the sake of showing the world we still matter. Luckily, Nick will be joining me on this trip, so I won't have to tolerate it alone.

I've become a master at tuning out the rhetoric, seeming engaged but completely detached from the conversation. In my ear, the translator gives me key points rather than a word-for-word playback. Something I'm grateful for. Nick sports an equally unamused expression, though you'd never know by looking at us how bored we really are. Another thing we picked up along the way during our royal duties. After all, it's all about appearances, as Mother would say.

"So, have you decided when you're going to spring the trap?" Nick asks once we return to our suite.

I shake my head. "It has to be soon though. Mother is acting strange and Gia is getting more stressed by the day. I don't know when it's safe to cross the line."

He nods and loosens his tie. "If it helps, all my things are lined up and ready whenever you are."

I clap his shoulder and smile. "Thank you. Truly. I can't tell you how much this means to me, having your support."

"It's what brothers do for each other." There's something else he's not telling me. "I met someone."

My eyes widen. "Really? Who?"

"No one you know."

I take a seat at the desk and raise a brow. "Oh no. You won't get off that easy."

He chuckles and shakes his head. "I met her at one of the foundation's events about six months ago."

Six months ago?

"Is she the reason for…?"

Nick nods, a slow smile spreading across his face. "She is."

How did he manage to keep this a secret for so long? But I've never seen him this happy. Something I can relate to. There's nothing better than the love of a woman.

"Congratulations," I say, engulfing him in a hug. "When do I get to meet her?"

He laughs and slaps my back. "All in due time. First, we have to solve your situation."

Don't remind me.

I glance at the clock. Gia should be giving me a call any minute. It's the one thing I've looked forward to during this trip. She sneaks away to take a break at the same time every night so we can FaceTime and see each other.

"Want to grab something to eat in a bit?"

Nick nods. "Sure. Tell Gia I said hi."

I smile and head to my room, eager to see my girl's face.

Five minutes.

Ten minutes.

Fifteen.

Where is she? Maybe she got caught up at the bar and couldn't get away. Although it's a weekday and shouldn't be too busy. But who knows when or why people go out to party or celebrate.

An hour ticks by and my nerves start to rise. Nick walks into the room, finding me sitting on the edge of the bed, willing my phone to ring.

"Are you okay?"

I look up and shake my head. "She hasn't called yet."

He sits next to me. "I'm sure she's busy. Come on, let's get some food in you so you won't pass out before she calls."

Good idea. Plus, it'll calm my mind and give me something else to focus on.

Only it doesn't help.

"It's been two hours and still no word from her," I say, pacing the floor of our living space. I'll be lucky if I have any hair left after tugging on it for so long.

"Why don't you give David a call, see if he knows something," Nick says, clasping his hands between his knees.

Yes. David would know.

Before my thumb pushes down on the number, his name

flashes across the screen. A sinking feeling fills my stomach, dread mixing with fear.

"David?" It's hard to make out where he is. Muffled sounds and noises fill the background as I wait for his answer. "David, what's going on?"

Finally, I hear him blow out a breath. "Sir, it's Ms. Hartley." The room spins as my worst fears are brought to the surface.

"What about Gia?" My voice shakes as I force the words from my mouth.

Nothing could prepare me for what he's about to say.

"There's been an accident."

CHAPTER
Eighteen

Gia

"What are you going to do on your day off?" Bryce asks as I wedge the phone between my ear and shoulder.

"No clue. With Luke out of the country and everyone else at work, guess I'll just bum around town for a bit. There's a shop I wanted to check out the other day. Now would be the perfect time."

Imagine my surprise when Matt told me I'd been working too hard and insisted I take a day off, even though I just had a week's vacation not that long ago. Apparently, even with a vacation, it's frowned upon to work seven days a week. I don't see a problem. Work keeps my mind busy.

"Good. Try to actually buy something, though." He knows me too well. I'm a horrible window shopper, too afraid to pull the trigger when push comes to shove. I still haven't decided on what I'm going to do. Mostly because I'm waiting to see what the endgame will be with Marguerite. Everything hinges on this plan succeeding. I don't have an exit strategy if everything goes to shit.

I laugh and check my purse once more to make sure I have everything I need for the day. "I make no promises."

Before he has the chance to rebut, I hang up and drop the phone in my bag. With the sun beating down and making it almost inhabitable outside, I opt for a pair of frayed shorts and tank top rather than my usual jeans and T-shirt. I guess it's one of the three days where the above-average temp keeps most normal people inside, but I love the sun and heat so I'm all about this weather. If I had a beach, I'd be set.

I gather my hair into a messy ponytail before locking my apartment and heading down the street, anxious to start my lazy day.

Between the in and out of air-conditioned stores and the hot sun beating down against the sidewalk, I'm in dire need of a break. Three stores, zero purchases. Bryce won't be happy, but he'll survive.

I scroll through my phone while sipping on a glass of chardonnay at a small café I've never been to with a cute little outdoor patio. As soon as I saw the caprese salad on the menu, I was sold.

The empty chair across from me screeches slightly as someone sits down, dropping a manila envelope onto the table.

"Ms. Hartley."

Simon.

Wonderful.

And here I thought I was going to be able to enjoy my day.

I set my phone in my purse and lean back. "What do you want?"

He grabs a passing waiter and orders me another glass of wine and a whiskey for himself. "You seemed lonely."

"Hardly."

"It's not often I see you outside during the day." He takes a sip of his drink, getting more comfortable in the chair. "Usually you're holed up in that shoebox of an apartment."

My heart kicks up a notch, but I tamp it down to school my features. I won't give him the satisfaction of knowing he's getting to me.

"You know, if you wanted to spend some time with me, all you had to do was ask. Not creepily stalk me all over."

His chuckle turns my stomach. "You're a funny girl. I can see why Prince Lucien is so enamored with you. Too bad your relationship will never survive."

I tilt my head to the side. "What relationship? Don't you read the papers? He's been seen with Kiera Wagner. They're the new power couple."

Simon stays silent, sipping his drink while holding my stare. "Power couple, eh?" He tosses the mysterious envelope my way. "Go ahead."

Ice cold dread grips my heart as I pick up the ominous, heavy package. What does he have in there?

Pictures.

Black and white.

Of me.

And Luke.

My chest constricts more as I flip through all the evidence he's collected over the last few weeks. Us at the bar. Sneaking into his house. The kissing incident in the hallway at the restaurant. The lodge. The club.

Everywhere we thought we were safe was captured on film.

No. We lost.

"As you see, it was a valiant effort on both your parts," he says, clapping his hands. "Your rouse of jilted lovers was cute and made for some wonderful headlines. However, Her Majesty was not quite as impressed when she received my report."

Shit. She already knows. I was hoping he was showing me these in exchange for his silence.

The pictures shake in my hands, feeling like a loaded gun with a hair-pin trigger.

"If you knew all along, why bother letting it go on?"

Simon takes another sip of his whiskey. "I needed something concrete. A few photos weren't enough to damage, but this collection here." He gestures to the stack still spread out on the table. "Well, as you can see, it's more than enough to show how long this has been going on. Show the lies and falsities you've pushed on the people."

I swallow thickly. Shit, is he threatening me with treason or something? How can me carrying on a relationship with the prince be treasonous?

"Nothing we did was illegal."

"No, it wasn't. You even got Prince Lucien to expedite your work visa paperwork so you wouldn't get deported."

"I never asked him to," I said, remembering Matt saying it'd been taken care of.

"You didn't have to. Manipulating a member of the royal family though, well…"

He lets his statement hang in the air, not needing to elaborate further.

I toss the photos onto the table, fighting to keep my slipping composure. "What do you want?"

A slow sneer creeps across his face. "Her Majesty believes you have overstayed your welcome. If you leave now, willingly and quietly, she won't drag you before the high court."

"You have no basis for any sort of hearing. It's her word against ours. Luke would never confirm her accusations."

"When given the choice between the crown or nothing, he will."

No. He wouldn't. I know he wouldn't.

Luke loves me, would stand up for me no matter what. It's why he devised this plan against his mom, trying to beat her at her own game. Only we didn't see this move coming.

I stay silent, trying to gather my thoughts together. Simon takes advantage and flags the waiter down, giving him a few bills to pay for everything.

"Consider it a departing gift." He stands from his chair, looking down his nose at me. "You have twenty-four hours. We know you'll make the right decision."

The minute he walks away, panic sets in. Did the air get thicker? Pain lances through my body, unable to stop the rush of emotion flooding to the surface.

What are we going to do?

Luke. I need to talk to him.

Gathering up the photos and shoving them into the envelope, I quickly dash from the café, heading back to my apartment.

The streets have gotten busier with the midafternoon traffic in full force.

I fumble through my purse while wiping away the tears. Damn it, where's my phone?

I don't see the stoplight turn green in the opposite direction.

A car horn blares to my right.

Everything falls to the ground as tires screech against the pavement, trying to halt the vehicle heading right at me.

But it's too late. Darkness falls over me as I succumb to my fate.

CHAPTER
Nineteen

Luke

"**W**here is she?" I storm the hospital help desk, not giving two fucks about the people waiting in line. As soon as David told me about the accident, I left the hotel and ran straight to the airport to board our private jet. Nick said he'd take care of everything and would meet me back in Lecara. The only thing on my mind was getting to Gia.

The poor receptionist's face pales for a second when she notices who I am.

"W-who, Your Highness?"

"Gia Hartley."

She nervously taps on the keyboard, drawing her brows together. "Um, s-she's on the fourth floor, south wing. But I'm not really allowed—"

There's no time to listen to her excuses. Not when my angel is hurt and I'm not there. My feet carry me as fast as they can down the hall, leaving my detail service in the dust as I hop on the first elevator I find.

She has to be okay.

She *needs* to be okay.

I won't entertain any other option.

Shocked gasps and glares aim at me as I burst through the door, the force causing it to bounce off the wall. Kendra and Bryce look up while Connor and Amelia stay huddled together on the couch. Reid paces back and forth in front of the large window overlooking the parking lot. Why are none of them in the room?

"What the hell happened?"

Bryce stands and places a hand on my shoulder. "We don't know exactly. It took us a while to find her and we haven't been allowed to go back to her room yet."

"What do you mean, you don't know? Why wasn't she at work?"

Reid stops pacing and joins us. "Matt gave her the day off since she was working too much."

"Why didn't anyone call me?"

Kendra wipes under her eyes. "The medics and police had a hard time identifying her. Apparently her phone was crushed in the accident and someone stole her purse, taking everything to show who she was."

David walks through the doors, holding his hat, Gia's purse, and an envelope in his hands. "I called as soon as I found out, sir. When I stopped at Ms. Hartley's apartment and didn't see the lights on, I went inside the bar and spoke with the owner, who stated he gave her the night off. It was unlike Ms. Hartley to not be home, so I did some digging and found out an unknown woman was injured several blocks away earlier and taken to the hospital. The police had recovered the stolen purse and called me since they've read the papers and knew you two had been close at one point. I then came straight here and after receiving some backlash from the staff, I was able to confirm it was Ms. Hartley. That's when I called you."

The room spins and sways, leaving my knees weak. But before I hit the floor, Reid ushers me to a nearby chair. Pain rips through my chest, making it hard to breathe.

Gia.

My angel.

"Luke, she'll be okay," Amelia says.

"I need to see her." I barely get the words out through the lump in my throat. This cannot be happening.

An older man in a white coat walks in. "Are you here for Ms. Hartley?"

Reid and Bryce lend me a hand, but I brush them off. "Yes, we all are. How is she?"

It takes everything I have to control the tremor in my voice. As a prince, I've been trained to withhold emotions, not show weakness. But my heart, my reason for being is lying in a hospital bed, injured and scared and alone. In this moment, I'm not a prince. I'm a man worried about the woman he loves.

The doctor nods as I approach. "Sir, she's doing fine. A few bumps and bruises, but nothing severe. We're keeping her in the hospital overnight for observation due to the mild concussion. She's lucky the car wasn't traveling very fast or things could have been worse."

She's okay. I repeat this mantra in my head while breathing a sigh of relief.

"Can I see her?"

He hesitates, looking at all our concerned faces, but nods. "One at a time, please."

The hallway is playing tricks on me. No matter how many steps I take, it seems to elongate and lengthen, keeping me away from my beloved. Each step echoes around us, aiding in the illusion.

We stop at a private room at the end of the hall. "I know you said one at a time, but I don't think I'll be able to leave her side once I get in the room."

Dr. Gutierrez, according to his name badge, smiles. "You're welcome to stay as long as she wants, Your Highness."

My heart thunders in my chest as I push through the door; the staunch scent of antiseptic assaulting my nostrils. There, in the bed next to a few monitors, is my angel.

I'm not sure how I manage to make it to her side as my feet feel like they're glued to the floor. Monitors beep and display numbers connected to various wires attached to her chest and fingers.

"Gia." My voice breaks as I perch myself on a nearby chair, grasping her hand in mine.

Until now, I thought our plan was foolproof. Nothing could touch us as long as we were together. This may be marked as an accident, but I know better. Somehow my mother is connected.

Gia stirs, squinting in pain while turning her head my way. "Lu-Luke."

Bringing her hand to my lips, I can't tear them away or break contact. Happiness and pain swirl together at hearing her voice.

"Angel." I cup her cheek with my available hand, taking note of the scrapes and bruises marring her beautiful skin. "I-I'm so sorry."

She tries to turn onto her side but can't. "It wasn't your fault."

"No, it was. I should have been here with you. This wouldn't have happened if I hadn't left."

"You-you can't think that," she says, weakly. "It wa-was an accident."

Nothing is ever just an accident. "Still, I should have been here to protect you."

A rogue tear slips down her cheek, tearing my heart in two at seeing her pain. "You're here now. That's what matters."

Without hesitation, I lean over her and press our lips together. Softly. Gently. Conveying my love and vow to protect her from now on.

"I would move heaven and earth to keep you safe."

"I know." She cups my cheek with sad eyes. "We lost."

Lost? "What do you mean?"

Tears flow freely down her cheeks now. "Simon... your mother... they know." Her voice hitches between words. "Th-there are pictures. Proof."

"The accident." Everything falls into place.

Her eyes widen. "N-no, they didn't have anything to do with it. After Simon left, I was digging through my purse to find my phone and didn't see the light change. The car came out of nowhere and I couldn't stop it."

"But Simon was the one who upset you." It wasn't a question.

Gia avoids my eyes. She doesn't need to confirm it. The hurt and suffering she's experienced will not go unpunished. People fear my mother's wrath.

Wait until she sees mine.

"Luke, I'm fine." Gia's voice pulls me back. I don't miss the wince as she tries to adjust her posture, placing a hand on one side of her ribs. "Let's not make this worse."

"You were hit by a car and are in a hospital bed, lucky to not have anything broken and being kept overnight for a concussion. If you think I'm going to ignore this, you're mistaken."

"I know," she says. "I know."

A knock sounds at the door before Reid pops his head through. "Is it okay if I come in?"

With a small nod and smile, Reid enters the room and pulls up a chair on the opposite side of the bed. Regret and pain briefly cross his face before he pushes them away.

"How are you feeling?"

Gia winces as she shrugs. "Like I got hit by a car."

"Funny," Reid says dryly. "You're a comedian."

"What can I say? I'm the life of the party."

Reid and I share a look. I know a slight amount of denial is normal after something traumatic, but she's not accepting what's happened. Brushing it off as if it wasn't a big deal?

"I'm going to step out for a moment and let you two have some privacy," I say, kissing her forehead before nodding at Reid. Maybe he'll be able to get through to her. Right now, I'm too emotionally connected to think clearly. Anger. Rage. Being so mad I want to hurt someone, anyone, just so they feel as helpless as I do right now.

She got hurt and I wasn't there to protect her.

Everyone picks their heads up as I walk back to the waiting room.

"How is she?" Kendra asks, picking her head up off Bryce's shoulder.

"She's cracking jokes and trying to make us believe it's not a big deal, so she'll be okay."

"Sounds like her," Bryce says. He stands and walks over, placing a hand on my shoulder. "How are you holding up?"

Excellent question. If only I knew how to answer it.

My nonresponse conveys more than words can as Bryce nods in understanding.

David walks over, still holding that damn envelope. "Sir, may I speak with you privately?"

Bryce excuses himself as we head to the hallway, away from the others. David's somber face instantly raises my guard.

He fumbles with the envelope. "This was found with Ms. Hartley's property. I think you should look at it."

An ominous, large manila envelope. I don't need to open it to know what I'll find. And just as I suspected, there—in black and white—are Gia and me on display when we thought we were being sneaky. Photo after photo after photo, raising my anger to levels I never thought possible.

"Has anyone else seen these?" I ask David, carefully shoving them back into the envelope.

David shakes his head. "No, sir. I confirmed it when I retrieved her property."

"Good. Keep this under tight watch." I hand it back to him.

"As you wish."

He turns to head back into the room, but I stop him before reaching the door. "David, there's something else I need you to do."

Once all our friends have gone home, I sneak back into Gia's hospital room. It will never get easier to see her lying in that bed. Even knowing she'll be okay doesn't stop the ache from tearing through my chest. Guilt is a horrible companion. It doesn't know when to go away or realize it's not actually your fault. Yet it sits like an unwanted houseguest, taking up residence in the back of your mind, tormenting you.

Thankfully, the hospital hasn't given me any flack for

spending the night in her room. Of course, a generous donation to their new expansion helped smooth the way.

I toe off my shoes and climb into the narrow bed, pulling her close to my chest. The last few hours have been hell, not being able to hold her, be next to her. Not in the way I want. Even with as close as we are now, it's not enough. The wires and IV lines, the constant glow of the monitors. All of it is a reminder of why she's here.

"I'm so sorry," I whisper against her hair, choking back the emotions trying to break free. Gia stirs in my arms, trying—and failing—to suppress a whimper. "Don't move, angel. You're hurt and in pain."

"It's getting better now that you're here." She wraps her arms around mine, absently running her fingers up and down my forearm. We stay silent for a while, the only noise coming from the hallway. "I can hear you thinking. What's on your mind?"

I hesitate, keeping my lips pressed to the back of her head. Talking about it makes it real, shows my failure.

"It's nothing," I say, taking the coward's way out.

Gia slowly turns in my arms, unable to lay on the other side due to her bruised ribs. Instead, she stays on her back, turning her head toward me while reaching up to gently stroke my cheek. Comforting me when she's the one hurt.

"Don't do that. Don't shut me out."

I turn my head and kiss her palm. "I'm just thankful you're alright."

"No, you're blaming yourself. I know you, Luke Claymore." She stares directly into my eyes. "Listen to me and listen good. You didn't cause this. It was an accident. Was I upset? Yes. But I wasn't paying attention. I'm at fault. If I had looked up, I would have noticed my surroundings, stayed on the sidewalk rather than walk directly into traffic. You do not get to carry this on your shoulders."

"I promised to protect you. Always."

She leans her forehead against mine. "You can't shelter me from the world. Things will happen. Good things. Bad things. And no one can stop them. You can't be glued to my hip twenty-four hours a day. What you're doing now, holding me, is perfect. This is how you can protect me. All you need to do is love me."

This woman constantly amazes me. Even with everything happening, she proves she's stronger than anyone else I know.

"With all that I am. Now and forever."

CHAPTER
Twenty

Luke

"**I**s everything set?"

David nods as he brings the car to the front of my house. It took everything I had to pull myself away from Gia this morning. After speaking with her doctors and them assuring me she won't be discharged for a few hours, I took the opportunity to shower at home and prepare for battle, using everything in my arsenal to attack my enemy with no mercy.

I have the high ground. And if there's one thing I've learned, it's to know your enemy. And I know her well. Know which moves she'll make, what tricks she'll try. But I hold all the cards. We're done playing games. Time to move in for the kill.

"Yes, sir."

"Good." I climb out of the car and head straight to my room, needing to put on my armor. A royal prince always looks the part. It's what she's told me my whole life. So dressing exactly as she expects, playing the perfect son is a start.

I walk to the main house, knowing who her first meeting of the day is with. If only she hadn't dragged the Wagner's into this mess. Even though Kiera assures me her father wasn't in on the plot, I can't verify it. On some level, he must have known.

"Sir, your mother is in a meeting and does not want to be disturbed." Thomas runs after me as I keep my focus on the doors.

"She won't mind."

He gasps at my shrewd response, stuttering nonsense as I push the grand doors open, finding my mother and Count Wagner seated across from each other in the parlor.

"Lucien. What's the meaning of this intrusion?" She stands, feigning disgust at the interruption.

"Forgive me, but this was urgent and could not wait." Count Wagner starts to stand, only to be halted when I raised a hand. "Please, stay. This also concerns you."

A tiny chip shows in her well-placed mask as her eyes widen with surprise. "Lucien, dearest, we don't need to concern the count with matters not pertaining to him."

I take a seat opposite them both, crossing a leg over my knee. "On the contrary, I believe it does."

Mother narrows her eyes; a tactic meant to intimidate. Normally it'd work, however, I'm immune to her threats. She preys on people's fears, cutting them down until they cave to her will. Unfortunately for her, that won't be happening. Not today. Not ever again.

The count looks between the two of us, his brows drawn tightly together. "I'm not entirely sure what's going on."

I fold my hands over my knee. "Allow me to enlighten you."

Right on time, Kiera walks through the doors with Thomas hot on her heels.

"I-I'm sorry, Your Majesty."

Mother waves him away. "Leave us." Putting her mask back into place, she puts on her fake smile as Kiera curtsies. "My dear, you look radiant this morning. To what do we owe this pleasure?"

Kiera sits next to me, at the ready for what's about to go down. "Thank you, Your Majesty. I was invited here by Prince Lucien for this highly important meeting."

Now her curiosity is piqued. "Oh? And why was I not informed of this meeting, rather to be ambushed during another."

"Please spare the dramatics. It's unbecoming of you," I respond, keeping my voice flat.

Her eyes widen again. "Lucien." Her voice holds a warning.

Poor Count Wagner looks between us and his daughter. "Can someone please explain?"

"Of course." Kiera stiffens her spine. "You've been holding a great number of private meetings with Queen Marguerite lately. We were wondering why."

His face pales slightly. "I, um, that is, we had important matters to discuss."

"Like what?"

He quickly looks to my mother, clearly unsure of how to proceed.

"It's a private affair. One that neither of you need to be concerned with," she says, saving him from lying to his daughter.

"I see. And this private affair wouldn't have anything to do with pushing the two of us together?" I say, waving a hand between myself and Kiera.

"As if we could control what you do. Honestly Lucien, how ludicrous of an idea."

"You're absolutely right. Which is why we caught on early to your little scheme."

"Scheme?" Mother lifts an eyebrow. "I have no idea what you're talking about. If anyone is scheming, it would be the two of you."

Kiera keeps her composure. "We were merely participating in the game."

Red starts to creep up my mother's neck. "There is no game. If anyone has been played, it would be the two of us. Posing for pictures, giving us hope for your union that would benefit everyone greatly. You should be thanking us for not exposing the farce of a relationship and turn you to the wolves of public opinion."

Kiera's father looks between the two of us, guilt clearly plaguing his thoughts. "We meant no harm."

Mother's head whips around quickly, a look of fear crossing his face under her scrutiny.

"So is that an admission for interfering in our lives?" I raise a brow in challenge.

True to form, she brushes an invisible piece of lint from her skirt and shakes her head. "Of course not. We simply placed the two of you together and let nature take its course. However, certain things needed to be taken care of."

My blood boils in my veins. "Certain things or a certain someone?"

Her lips curl into a sinister sneer. "I don't know what you mean."

"Am I to assume that Simon conveniently showing up where I'm at is a coincidence? Or his constant stalking of Gia?"

The air in the room chills at the mention of her name. It's not a surprise she knows I know of her spy. If she wanted to keep it a secret, he would have been more discrete. However, she was flaunting her power, trying to prove she was in charge.

"Must we talk about that girl? Honestly, I don't understand

why she's still here or why you care after the way she hurt and publicly humiliated you."

I clench my fists at my sides. "If anyone should be humiliated here, Mother, it's you. After all, this whole thing started that night. Isn't that right, Count Wagner?"

He looks between the three pairs of eyes staring at him. I wonder where his loyalties lie: with his daughter or with the evil queen.

"I-I," he stutters before swallowing hard. "It may have come up the night of the gala that a relationship and eventual marriage between the two of you would be advantageous for everyone involved."

And there it is. The motive I couldn't quite figure out. "What would you have gotten out of this?"

Kiera waits for her father's answer, holding her breath. "Land. Not to mention a seat at the royal cabinet, in addition to joining our bloodline into the royal family." His eyes soften as he looks at his daughter. "It's what you wanted."

"Never," Kiera says, scoffing. "I never said that."

He tilts his head, dropping the innocent façade. "Nonsense. Ever since you were little, you wore crowns and tiaras, claiming that one day you'd sit on the throne."

"That was make-believe! A child's imagination. All little girls dream of being a princess."

"Even as a teenager?"

Kiera grits her teeth. "I won't deny my crush on Lucien. Part of me wanted to pursue a relationship, but not at the expense of our friendship. When it was made perfectly clear he was off the market for good, it was enough for me to come to grips with reality."

"Off the market? Lucien has never been off the market," Mother exclaims.

I lean forward, resting my elbows on my knees. "Yes, I have.

For months now. Just because you're incapable of accepting it doesn't make it any less true."

She scoffs. "That American girl? She's not worthy of such a luxury."

"Why? Because she's not from here?"

Her patience is fleeting, barely clinging on by a thread. "I don't need to explain my reasoning to you. This union between the two of you is perfect. With Nicolai assuming the throne soon, your father and I won't have to worry about the stability of our house."

"But why worry about my marriage? Why not focus on Nick since he's the heir apparent?"

She smirks as if I asked the dumbest question on earth. "Nicolai will marry whoever we choose. He's loyal to the crown and would never jeopardize our heritage by muddying the waters with foreign blood."

Muddying the waters? Rage like I've never felt before courses through me like wildfire. She has the audacity to sit there and pass judgment on a woman she hasn't taken the time to get to know. All because she doesn't come from some noble blood-line, something that doesn't even matter anymore. This isn't the Middle Ages. Hell, it's not as if we're really needed by the public other than to fill some long-standing tradition. The royal family is more for show than anything else.

I stand abruptly, ready to bring down the house when the doors swing open, revealing a very angry Nick storming into the room.

"Nicolai!" Mother gasps, clearly thrown by this new intrusion. "Wha-what are you doing here?"

Finally, we caught her off guard. "I'm here to right some wrongs."

Not one to show weakness, she slides her mask firmly into place. "Darling, this doesn't concern you. This is a minor disagreement between your brother and I, who unfortunately has also dragged the Wagner's into this mess."

"Mother, please. I know all about the situation," he says, taking a seat next to me, "and I'm here to tell you the situation has changed."

She quirks a brow. "I'm not sure I know what you mean."

"I heard it all. How unconcerned you are about my station since I follow your word blindly." Nick leans back; a smug look creeping across his face. "Well, let me enlighten you on the current events happening under your nose."

I look over to Kiera, who sports an equally amused grin.

Showtime.

"And what events would that be?" Mother nervously darts her eyes to Count Wagner then back to her favorite son.

"My abdication."

She sits there, stunned silent, trying to process what my brother announced. Something directly opposite of her plans. Something she never thought would happen.

And I can't help but smile.

"You-your what? Nicolai, you don't know what you're saying."

Nick acts like he hasn't turned her world upside down. "Oh, but I do. I've decided that my foundation would be better served without my constant absence. I could do more for millions of people without being tied down to your agendas. Other royals have done it. Now I'm taking a page from their book. I'm tired of being your puppet."

Red creeps up her face, practically turning it an ungodly shade of purple. I've seen her mad before, but never like this.

"No, I don't accept this. You cannot do this to your father, to me, to the crown and its people."

Nick looks to me with a nod. "Actually, it's done. After your little display the last few weeks, you've proven that what we want is irrelevant. Our happiness means nothing to you."

"You are the crown prince of Lecara. Happiness is not necessary for your duties. Both you and your brother have lost sight of what's important."

"No, we know exactly what's important," I say. "Finding the balance between love and happiness while doing what's best for everyone, including the people we serve. We both have found our life's purpose and I support Nick's decision to step down. Now the question, dear mother, is whether or not you'll accept our conditions."

She sits back in her chair, silently brooding while taking inventory of her losses. "And what demands are those?"

Of course she has to be difficult. "First, you accept Nick's abdication and let him do his life's work how he wants to do it." When she doesn't respond, I continue. "Second, you accept Gia and drop this ridiculous vendetta against her."

"No." She says it with the utmost finality, daring us to challenge her authority.

I glance to Kiera, who nods and heads to the door. Both our parents watch with rapt attention, their eyes widening when she returns with Miriam in tow.

Mother darts her gaze to me, a sneer forming once again. "What's going on here?"

"Marguerite." There's no warmth in Miriam's greeting. "I'm here to advocate on behalf of Gia who is unable to speak for herself at the moment."

"And why would she need someone to step in for her?"

Miriam raises a brow. "Surely you cannot be so daft and tell me you did not know that Ms. Hartley has been in the hospital since yesterday after being confronted by your little spy."

No one has ever spoken that way to her before, as was evident by her expression. "Are you implying I had something to do with her accident? Do you know who you are speaking to?"

"I do," Miriam says, stepping closer. "My oldest friend. Someone I used to respect because of her compassion for people from all walks of life. Did you forget where we came from? How your current circumstances came to be? Has it been so long that you forgot you were once a regular woman, enamored by the love of your life?"

"We were different. Both of us were noble women, destined for greatness."

Miriam scoffs. "And who's to say Gia isn't? Do you think it was chance or luck that Lucien met her or that she came to Lecara?"

"No, that was the doing of your sons."

"It was fate. Your denial and excuses mean nothing. How do you not see what the rest of us do when we look at the two of them together?"

Unfortunately, Miriam's words fall on deaf ears. "She's not worthy. There's no possible way she can handle the responsibility of the position."

"How would you know unless you give her a chance?"

The doors behind us swing open, causing everyone's head to turn. My father strides confidently into the room, anger radiating off him in waves. I've seen this look before. Only once. It was also the last time someone had dared to challenge his authority.

"Marguerite, you sound like a petulant child." Everyone stands and bows, showing their respect. "I've sat by idly, listening to your words, hoping you would make the right decisions regarding our sons and safeguarding the needs of the country. However, I cannot tolerate these actions any longer and let you continue on this course."

She looks around the room, trying to find any sort of support, only to be greeted by the emotionless faces of those who were wronged by her actions. "My dear, I think there's been a misunderstanding."

"Only on your part. I've spoken with Nicolai and granted his abdication, putting Lucien in line for the crown." He turns to me with compassionate eyes. "And I'm to assume if your mother does not drop this vendetta against Ms. Hartley, you also will abdicate, letting our royal line end."

I nod. "That is my intention, yes."

Turning again to his wife, he frowns. "And you know who will be the next successor. Do you want that for this country you supposedly love?"

The room stills as our words finally sink in.

Game. Set. Match.

Father turns his attention to Kiera, who has stayed silent during this whole endeavor. "I apologize for the queen's actions. Believe me, they were not meant to intentionally hurt you."

"It's all right, Your Majesty. I only want what's best for Lucien."

He nods, turning his attention to her father. "I'm willing to overlook this deception on the condition it will *never* be spoken about again, nor will the actions be repeated."

Count Wagner pales and hangs his head. "Of course, Your Majesty. I sincerely apologize for any misdeeds on my part and vow to—"

Father raises a hand, cutting off his speech. "Yes, good."

Finally, he turns to me, placing a hand on my shoulder. "Is Ms. Hartley all right?"

I nod. "Some bruised ribs and a mild concussion, among other things, but she's okay. The doctors say she'll be discharged this afternoon."

"Good. Make the necessary arrangements for all her belongings to be moved to your residence immediately. She will still need to be watched and I won't allow her to live alone while recuperating."

I smile, thankful he's on our side. "Already done."

He nods and smiles. "She is a good woman and will make a fine future queen for our country."

To have his approval means the world. Mother slinks over, her tail tucked between her legs. "Frederick, I think—" She doesn't have the chance to complete her sentence as my father cuts her off with a raise of his hand.

"We will discuss your actions later. For now, you are no longer allowed to interfere with our children's lives. You will accept their choices because they deserve to be happy. And if I hear of one more incident, there will be dire consequences."

Knowing she's lost, she nods her head and looks between Nick and me. "You have my word."

Kiera catches my eye, shooting me a victorious grin. Miriam also shows her approval.

We did it. It's over. Nick and I are finally free to live our lives the way we want without fear of repercussion.

"Thank you, father," I say. He only nods and escorts my mother out of the room.

It feels as if a weight has been lifted off my shoulders. All the trials and tribulations, the secret meetings and sneaking around were worth it.

Miriam takes my hand in hers. "Congratulations, my boy. I'm excited for this next chapter in your life."

She's been like a second mother to me, encouraging without judgment my entire life. I couldn't have asked for a better ally. "Thank you, Miriam. For everything."

"Always happy to help." With a quick maternal kiss to my cheek, she turns to leave.

Count Wagner looks to Kiera and me, his face filled with regret. "Again, Your Highness, I apologize for my actions."

"Like my father said, it's never to be mentioned again. I won't be one to hold a grudge over this incident. As far as I'm concerned, it's over and done with."

He nods and leaves the room, hanging his head to avoid eye contact.

Kiera runs up to me, throwing her arms around my waist and squeezing tight. "Congratulations, Lucien."

I return the gesture. "Are you okay?"

She nods and steps back. "My father will have a lot of apologizing to do, but I'll be okay. Besides, I have my new career to focus on now that I'm not being dragged to unnecessary functions anymore."

Nick laughs. "I know the feeling."

"I'm glad everything worked out for the best. For all of us."

"Me too." Without another word, she gives a small wave and leaves the two of us alone.

"When did you talk with father?" It's the question that's been nagging me since he walked into the room.

"About an hour ago. I knew she wouldn't accept our demands, so I figured we needed a bigger gun."

I laugh. "That was quite the gamble."

He shrugs. "I knew he'd be more accepting of the

circumstances than she would. And he doesn't share her views on Gia. He's actually quite fond of her."

"Really?" He's never once let on about his opinion of her. Always stayed silent and stoic whenever her name was mentioned in my company. Then again, you'd have an easier time discovering the secrets of the universe than reading his thoughts.

"We all are," Nick says, clapping my shoulder. "You will make an excellent king one day." A bittersweet smile crosses his face. For so long, he's been prepared for the throne, to take on the responsibility passed down from generation to generation. Yet, there's also relief in knowing he can do so much good for so many people. "Oh, father also wanted you to have this." He slips a small square box into my hand. "When the time is right."

My heart practically leaps in my chest, knowing what's inside. His acceptance of my relationship means everything.

"Thank you," I say, hugging my first best friend.

He chuckles before pulling back. "If you screw this up, I will come back and make you regret it."

"Not a chance."

I slide the box into my pocket and give Nick a final nod before sending David a text to ready the car.

There's someone I need to bring home. For good.

CHAPTER
Twenty-One

Gia

"Luke, I'm perfectly capable of taking care of myself."

No matter how much I try, my pleas fall on deaf ears as the car pulls up in front of his house.

"This is a direct order from the king. Would you like to tell him no?"

I clamp my lips together and shake my head. Damnit. Considering everything we've been through, I'm not about to make waves.

Luke told me how things went down with his parents earlier today and I couldn't believe how everyone rallied to our cause. Between Nick, his dad, even Miriam, I'm forever in their debt. The relief of not needing to hide was better than learning I sustained no major injuries yesterday after the accident.

"That's what I thought." Luke places a gentle kiss on my lips before guiding me out from the back seat of the car. Placing his hand in mine, we make our way to his bedroom, saying hello to the various staff members wandering around.

"What the?"

Why is all my stuff here?

Luke shrugs and drags me farther into the room. "Again, the king's orders."

How long is he going to use that line? "Maybe I should have a talk with the king to verify your words."

He pulls me close, pressing our lips together while running his hands up and down the curves of my body.

I've missed our closeness, our intimacy since we've had to hide and pretend we're not together. Now that we're free, there's nothing stopping us from being who we are with each other. The way we were in Chicago. Two carefree souls destined to be together, no matter what the world throws at us.

"Do you really want to discuss my father while alone in our room?"

I pull back and quirk a brow. "Our room?"

He's so cute when he blushes. It's not often since nothing ever gets to him, but when it happens, it's adorable. It makes him seem younger, like a little kid.

Luke leads me to the bed, setting me down gingerly. "I know I should have asked, but I can't be away from you anymore. One thing I've learned over the past few weeks is that I won't take things for granted. Stealing moments with you wasn't enough and I won't do it anymore." His gentle touch ignites a fire across my cheek, spreading warmth throughout my body even though I'm not cold. In fact, I'm quite the opposite. Every touch, every look, every breath shared between us leaves me burning for more. I will never get enough of this man.

But I'm not about to stop his little speech now.

He tucks a few strands of hair behind my ear, letting his fingers linger against my skin while dragging them slowly down the column of my throat. I close my eyes and try to control my breathing. There's still some lingering pain in my ribs, though it's mostly controlled through the pain meds the doctor gave me. However, it's getting harder to control myself when he touches me this way. I could curse the doctor for saying sex is off the table for a few days to give my body time to heal. I don't think he understands that I'm not in control when Luke is around. Instinct takes over and it doesn't care about bumps and bruises.

But I know Luke does.

I suck in a hiss as he brushes his hand across a sensitive part of my side.

Fine. Maybe the doctor was right.

"I'm sorry, angel." His eyes hold mine with an unspoken apology.

I reach up and cup his cheek. "There's no need to apologize." I pull him closer, skimming my lips across his, teasing him until he opens to give me access to deepen the kiss.

Before we have the chance to take it beyond what we can, a knock sounds at the door, pulling us apart.

"Yes?" I try not to laugh at Luke's annoyed expression at the unwanted interruption.

One of his house staff steps through the door, bowing slightly. "Your Highness, forgive the intrusion, but a delivery has arrived for Ms. Hartley."

I knit my brows together. "For me?"

Luke smiles and helps me stand. "Thank you. Please send it in."

"What delivery?" I ask once we're alone again.

Luke only smiles and kisses the tip of my nose. "Some things I thought you needed."

Nothing good ever comes from that phrase when he says it.

The doors open again, this time with multiple people carrying in box after box, placing each one on the floor by the closet. My eyes practically bulge from their sockets. Does this parade ever end?

Finally, the last one is set down, leaving us alone with a small fortress of things to unpack. I shoot Luke a glare. The jerk only smiles and shrugs.

"Looks like you'll have to open them to find out."

I carefully head over to the first box I don't have to bend down to open. Something tells me *His Highness* will be doing most of the unpacking.

It can't be.

The stuff I left behind at the Whittaker Manor.

"But how? Why?"

Luke slides his hands along my hips, mindful of my injuries. "Miriam and I decided that you no longer needed the room, so I arranged to have everything brought here."

This man. So sweet and thoughtful, yet frustrating and stubborn at the same time.

"Honestly, I didn't need all these things. I was going to return them to Kendra."

He leans down to whisper in my ear. "She refused to take them. And you deserve to have them in your section of the closet."

"My section?" I twist my head to the side, bringing him into my peripheral. "And how big is this section? Judging by the number of boxes, I may need an entire room to myself."

Goose bumps coat my skin as his lips graze the slope of my shoulder, trailing up my neck until his warm breath tickles my ear. "Angel, I will give you whatever your heart desires."

Ugh, that voice. Why did he have to use his sex appeal voice, especially since there's nothing we can do about it? Not that it would matter. The man could recite the phone book and it'd still make me wet and needing more.

A low moan erupts from the back of my throat as his fingers skim up my waist, brushing against the sides of my breasts, careful not to use too much pressure. Instead, it has the opposite effect; pebbling my nipples until they're so hard the only thing to soothe the ache are his lips wrapped around them.

My breathing accelerates, want morphing to need as I focus on his lips while pushing my ass against his erection.

"Luke." My voice is breathy and quiet, not hiding my true desire.

"Angel," he says into my ear. "There is nothing more I'd love to do right now than christen every inch of this house, watching you come over and over until every surface has your scent ingrained into the very fiber of the foundation." A chill runs down my spine, failing to diminish the fire burning inside. "But not yet. Once you are in the clear, be prepared for several days of making up to do."

"And the staff?"

He stealthily cups my breasts, feeling their heavy weight in his palms while easing some of the ache he created. I hiss slightly at the sharp pain from my side, proving that we're not ready to do anything physical yet.

"We will be all alone. I don't share things that are most precious to me." Luke turns me in his arms, cradling my face in his hands. "And you, angel, are mine and mine only."

A slow smile creeps along my face. "I like the sound of that."

He kisses my forehead, my cheeks, my nose, then finally my lips. "As do I." With a lingering kiss, we step apart and try to cool down our bodies.

I look around at the mess and crack my knuckles. "Looks like we have some organizing to do."

Rather than dig through the boxes, Luke grabs me by the shoulders and sets me on the edge of the bed. "Not quite. You're supervising. I'm unpacking."

Like I said, stubborn.

After sitting around for the last few weeks, it feels good to get back to normal as I put the finishing touches on my makeup. Nothing much, but since Luke and I are officially a thing in the public, I figured I should probably put more of an effort into my appearance. There's no way those papers are going to be right about the harlot American girl who stole the prince's heart.

Luke slides his hands around my hips, pulling me into the safety of his chest. More importantly, without making me smudge my eyeliner.

"You look so sexy right now, standing here with practically nothing on."

No one said I couldn't be a harlot in private with him, though. It may have been my intention to tease him with the black lace bra and thong set as I get ready for work. Something I've been looking forward to. Luke, not so much. He wants to keep me locked away in the safety of his home, even though I keep telling him I wasn't run down in the street. The bruises have finally faded, removing any trace of the accident, which has helped ease his guilty conscience.

His hands roam over my body, sending little electric charges through my skin. I close my eyes on a gasp as he cups a breast with one hand while trailing the other down my stomach, letting it settle between my legs.

"You're going to make me late," I say, leaning into his touch and handing over whatever control I had.

Our eyes meet in the mirror, passion and desire hanging heavy around us.

We both knew I was never going to be on time in the first place. Once the doctor gave me the all-clear for physical activity, it was game on. I'm honestly surprised he agreed when I told him I needed to get out and work tonight.

"I can be quick." He nibbles on my ear while brushing his finger against my clit.

A deep-seated burn flickers to life as I hold his gaze. "We both know that's a lie." Just to add to the torture, I rub my ass against his hardening cock, still confined within his jeans.

Maybe I won't give up all my control.

Only he uses my move to his advantage, slipping a finger under the flimsy lace, feeling how excited and ready I am. We haven't had a drought this long since he left Chicago. Three weeks of wanting and needing, being so close to each other and unable to do anything about it has been torture.

That all stops right now.

Luke makes quick work of his pants. I grin as I hear the belt buckle thud against the marble floor.

"Keep your eyes on mine, angel."

He slides the material to the side, easing himself inside me.

God, I've missed this, being intimate with the man I love. Every touch, every move, every look sends me reeling, filling a void that completes me without even knowing I was missing anything.

I brace my hands on the counter, keeping my eyes on his as he picks up speed. It's hard not to close them and give in to the pleasure he so easily pulls with each stroke. Luke grips my hips tighter, pulling me back to find a spot deep inside, eliciting a long moan that echoes around the room.

"Ha-harder," I pant out. Protectiveness and raw, animalistic desire struggle for dominance as he chews on his bottom lip, clearly at war with letting himself go versus protecting me. "I'm not a delicate flower. You won't break me. Now fuck me like you want me."

His eyes darken, the black nearly taking over the blue as he pulls my hips back more while propping my right leg on the counter, completely opening me up to him. Somehow he manages to slip in deeper, hitting spots I never knew existed.

One of his hands glides up my throat, cradling my jaw in his palm while he digs his fingertips on the other into my hip. There will probably be bruises tomorrow, but who cares. The only person who will see them is the one making them.

"Fuck. Angel. Fuck." He punctuates each word with a sharp thrust, bringing me closer to the edge. Thank God no one can hear us. They'd probably send in the police thinking I was being murdered. Though I won't rule out death by orgasm.

The very essence of sex fills the room; our musky scent and the sound of our skin slapping together only gets me more excited. I do my best to hold off on the orgasm knocking at the door, knowing it's practically impossible as my toes start to curl on their own.

"Do it," he growls low in my ear. "I know you're there." Just to make sure, his fingers abandon my hip and find my swollen clit, pressing down hard as I lose control.

"Oh god!" I chant over and over as white-hot pleasure rips through my body while he keeps us facing the mirror, unable to look away at the spectacle we've become.

"Look at how sexy you are when you come all over my cock."

He doesn't slow down, keeping his punishing pace until a second orgasm rocks me to my core, leaving me a shaking, quivering mess in his arms.

Keeping his eyes on mine, he speeds up, turning his movements shaky. "Fuck, Gia. Fuck!" With a few last jerks, he empties himself into me, pressing his chest into my back while biting down slightly on my shoulder.

Holy shit, we both needed that.

We take a moment to calm down before easing ourselves into an upright position. My right hip aches from being held up but I'd gladly take that any day of the week if it meant Luke was giving me multiple orgasms at once.

I turn in his arms and plant a kiss on his lips, teasing and sucking the bottom one until I feel him smile against me.

"Thank you for not smudging my makeup."

Luke raises a brow. "That's all you're thanking me for?"

I hop up on the counter and pull him closer, wedging his body between my legs. "And the two screaming orgasms."

He runs a hand through my hair, and I find myself getting lost in those blue pools, reflecting the love and affection I feel for him right back at me. "I love you, angel of mine."

His words remind me of the song that played in the Uber after our first night together. "I love you, too." With a final kiss, I push him back so I can hop back on the ground. "Now we need to get cleaned up again so we can go out."

Thank God Matt was super understanding about my tardiness. Then again, it's highly suggested not to argue with the prince when he says he's at fault for an employee being late.

"Have I told you you're the best boss ever?"

He looks over with a sideways grin. "We'll see if you're whistling the same tune later."

Why would it change? "Is there a big crowd coming in that you didn't tell me about?"

He glances over my shoulder and shrugs. "I have a feeling tonight could get interesting."

Geez, vague much? "What aren't you telling me?"

Without answering my question, he tosses me a rag and word-lessly points to the opposite end of the bar. Looks like this will be my station for the night. Unfortunately, it's far away from Luke and everyone else who is gathered at the usual table.

Kendra spots me instantly and bounds over, bringing several empty glasses at the same time. "Gia, I'm so glad you're here. The boys are running low."

"Uh huh, sure. *The boys.*" Grabbing the empty mugs and putting them in the dishwasher, I fill up a new round before sliding them her way. "And what about you?"

"Oh, I still have my drink at the table. Why on earth does Matt have you down here?"

Isn't that the question of the day. "Beats me. Maybe there is a girl he likes on the other end. Or this is my punishment for Luke making me late."

"Bet you'd let him make you late all the time if you have the choice," she says with a wink.

Not wrong, but I won't admit it out loud at the moment. Too many ears present. Just because we're officially a couple doesn't mean I want to give the tabloids any juicy fodder to print about us.

"Try not to forget about me tonight."

A slow smirk plays on her lips. "Not going to happen."

Before I have the chance to ask her to elaborate, she skips off with the drinks. Why is everyone speaking in code tonight? It's like a horrible game of telephone and I'm the person on the end with half the information.

People keep swarming into the bar, keeping Matt and I running like crazy to fill everyone's drink order. It's strange, though, since everyone is staring at me but quickly avert their eyes as soon as I notice. Is it really that weird for the prince to be dating a commoner? I'd like to think in this day and age it's more normal. Not everyone shared the queen's view on our relationship. Once word got out, my Instagram and Facebook blew up with followers. People were messaging me, telling me how lucky I was—or that I was an unworthy bitch. Not a lot of middle ground. It got to be so much I had to shut both of them down, which was suggested by the palace anyway.

I look over to Matt, who clears out four chairs at his end of the bar, slapping a reserved sign in front of them.

What the fuck? We don't reserve seats here.

With the crowd so thick, I can barely see my friends anymore. Every time I try to look over the sea of people on my tiptoes, my side starts to ache and I have to stop. Maybe Luke was right. I should have taken an extra day or two to rest up and fully heal. Then again, I wouldn't have had amazing bathroom sex earlier.

It's a give and take.

"Gia!" Matt waves me down as I slide some money into the cash register. "Can you cover for me real quick? I've got to grab something in the back."

Sweat drips down the side of my face as I pull on the front of my shirt, trying to get any sort of ventilation I can. "Yeah, sure."

How long is he going to be gone? And what on earth would he need to grab? Everything is well stocked and we haven't touched the backup supply yet.

I'm wiping down a section of counter when a shadow casts over the now-clean spot. "Hey, can you do me a favor?"

I know that voice. One I haven't heard in a couple months and I've missed. Sure enough, I look up and see Angie's smiling face beaming at me.

"Oh my god, Ang!" I practically crawl over the counter to throw my arms around her neck, squeezing her like my life depended on it. "How did you… when did you… what are you doing here?"

She smirks and her eyes flit to the side. "I have a few guys that have a reservation. Can I put them in your section?"

Did the plane ride fry her brain? "Um, Angie, you don't work here. What are you talking about?"

"They're here for a bachelor party and requested to sit at the bar."

Slowly, realization dawns on me. The very first night Luke and I met she said something similar, putting everything into motion for the wildest ride of my life.

"Yeah, I can take them."

Angie jerks her head to the side where Matt had placed the reserved placard. "Well, go on."

"We're talking later," I say, giving her hand a quick squeeze before making my way to the four men sitting at the end, sporting similar outfits from the night we met.

"Hey guys, welcome to the Bull and Boar. My name's Gia. What can I get for you?"

Reid smiles, folding his arms over each other. "I'll have an IPA."

Bryce smirks. "I'll have a cream ale."

"Still a pansy," Connor says. "IPA for me."

My heart stills as I stare into Luke's eyes, now shielded behind those sexy, black-rimmed glasses, stripping me down until there is nothing left. Just like I wanted that first night but couldn't say.

"Ladies' choice." The smooth, sensual timbre of his voice practically has my knees knocking to match my thundering heart.

"Awfully brave, leaving such an important decision to someone else."

He leans forward to grasp my hand and bring it to his lips. Tingles zing up and down my arm at the slight contact. It feels as if everyone is focused on us. I can practically feel their burning gazes while my own cheeks heat and flame.

"Beautiful women are never wrong."

Still just as smooth as ever.

He reluctantly releases my hand, allowing me to grab their drinks. That's when I notice a few familiar faces standing behind them.

Next to Angie is Callie, smiling brightly while leaning her head against Max's shoulder. My parents are behind them with my mom dabbing a tissue under her eyes. Hell, even my sister Lisa and her husband are here.

What in the...?

I set the drinks down and nervously chew on my bottom lip. "S-so what brings you guys in tonight?"

Reid smiles. "A bachelor party."

"Oh?" My stomach flips and turns like the entire Olympic gymnastics team is inside practicing. "Who's the lucky bachelor?"

Reid looks to Bryce, who looks to Connor, who flashes me the widest grin I've ever seen before turning his head to Luke. "This guy."

The entire room goes silent as Luke stands from the stool and quickly rounds the bar. A million spasms seize the muscles in my chest. This is it. I'm officially having a heart attack.

Tilting my head up, I stare into the love of my life's eyes. I try to open my mouth to say something while not looking like a fish gasping for breath, only nothing comes out.

Luke presses a finger to my lips. "Gia, from the moment I met you, I knew you were someone special. You showed your capacity for kindness when you agreed to take four complete strangers on a tour of your hometown without ever asking for anything in return. Those three days were some of the best in my life. Our seamless connection and easy conversations made it obvious that I needed to know more about you and I'm grateful to Bryce and Connor every day for bringing you here." He cradles my cheek in his warm palm. A rogue tear slips from my eye, which he easily brushes away with his thumb. "You're the best surprise wrapped in this spunky, fiery package, unafraid to stand up for what she believes in and fight for what she wants. All the qualities of someone to look up to. Heaven knows I do."

"Luke." I barely get the word out since my voice has stopped working.

Time stands still as Luke drops to a knee on the sticky bar mat, grabbing my hands in his on the way down. "For the first time in my life, I have a clear picture of what I want and who I want to share it with. And so, Gianna Katherine Hartley, will you do me the great honor of standing by my side and becoming my wife?"

He pulls out a small box from his pocket, opening it up to reveal a huge princess-cut diamond surrounded by a myriad of smaller ones, practically glowing from the overhead lights.

This man. This crazy, amazing, selfless man wants to spend his life with me. Knowing what I do about how his life will play out, the trials and tribulations we'll face, the lack of privacy and potential threats… I won't even touch on his mother. None of it would push me away from spending my entire life by his side.

"Yes," I whisper, surprised any sound came out. "Of course I'll marry you."

In one fell swoop, he lifts me off my feet and kisses me like no one's watching, even though the thunderous applause and numerous flashes of light say otherwise. My childhood dreams come true as he slips the ring on my finger. It glimmers and shines, and more surprisingly, it is a perfect fit.

"It was my grandmother's ring. My father gave it to me because he knew you were the one."

Once again I'm stunned silent. To have such a precious family heirloom on my hand, knowing it has been passed down from generation to generation means the world to me. Except I'm so afraid I'll drop it down the bathroom sink or lose it in some tragic and horrible fashion. It is me, after all.

"How did you do all this?" Not that I doubt his ways. He's a hard person to say no to, even if he wasn't royalty. There's something about his charisma that draws you to him, willing to obey any request or command.

"Angel, I'd do anything for you. And a moment like this deserved to be shared with your family and friends."

On cue, my mother runs over and pulls me out from behind the bar while practically squeezing the life out of me. "Gia, I'm so happy for you. It's been so hard keeping this a secret for the last few weeks."

Few weeks? I know I've been slightly out of touch since the accident, but wow, how did I miss this? But it means the world to me that Luke knew I would want my family and friends here to witness this momentous event.

"I'm so glad you're here, Mom."

She kisses my cheek before turning the same attention to Luke. "He's a good man. You hold on to him tight and don't let go."

Lacing our fingers together, I look into his eyes and smile, seeing my future play out in those gorgeous blue irises.

"Never."

What started as a vacation fling has turned into the best decision of my life. I can't imagine not spending my life with Luke. And now I'm glad I never have to.

Maybe this was a storybook fairy tale after all.

Epilogue

Reid

Tonight was perfect. Luke really is quite the romantic at heart. I blame it on his pedigree. Women love that sappy shit, all hearts and flowers and promises of forever. It's why romance novels and movies are a billion dollar a year industry. Everyone wants to find love.

Only that industry has painted a very unrealistic picture.

Not everything falls perfectly into your lap. Sometimes you need to work for it. Or open your eyes to possibilities that weren't there before.

Jealousy drove me to try and take Gia away from Luke. How stupid was that? Anyone can plainly see how in love they are with one another.

Everyone is milling about the pub, chatting about this or that, laughing and admiring the ring sitting proudly on Gia's finger.

I am happy for them. Truly. But the guilt I feel at the pain

I caused will never go away. They say they've forgiven me and I should be grateful. The question is, do they trust me anymore?

"Matt, whiskey, neat." He nods his head and grabs a bottle from the top shelf, pouring it with a flourish in front of me.

"Quite the night, eh?"

I take a sip, letting the burn crawl down my throat before answering. "It's fitting for them. Gia deserves the fairy tale."

"That she does," he says with a smile. "I'm just sad to see my favorite bartender go."

Right. Because she's going to become a princess.

Someone calls for his attention at the other end of the bar, leaving me alone with my thoughts again. I spin on the stool, taking in the crowd. Or as Gia calls it, people watching. I never understood the fascination, but as I sit here and take in the moment, I get it.

Only one person catches my eye. The beautiful brunette sitting at a table across the room, laughing at something Kiera said while clinging to her brother Bryce's shoulder.

I can't help but stare at the joy spread across her face, looking carefree and happy. A sudden image assaults my mind, bringing me back to a memory that is replayed almost daily.

Kendra's laugh echoes down the quiet hallway as we stumble out of the elevator, bracing ourselves against the wall for stability.

"Shh, you're going to get us in trouble," I say, holding her up by the waist.

She smiles and looks at me with those chocolate brown eyes. "Since when are you afraid of a little trouble?"

When we left Luke and Gia's room, she wasn't ready to call it a night and I wasn't about to let her go to the bar in the condition she was in. So I tagged along to keep her company and out of trouble. One drink turned to three, which turned into staying until bar close.

"Reid, can I ask you something?" She leans against the wall by her door, twisting her fingers together.

I join her against the wall, shoving my hands into my pockets. "Sure."

"Have you ever been in love?"

Her question takes me by surprise. "I'm not sure. Maybe?" With the whiskey fogging my brain, it's hard to remember anything, let alone feelings from the past.

Sadness clings to her smile as she leans against my shoulder. "I have. Or I thought I was."

Really? I hardly remember Kendra ever having a serious relationship. "When?"

"For years I was in love with this guy, but he never knew. Or maybe he did and never felt the same way. Definitely one-sided."

Having just experienced it myself, I can relate. "Did you ever try to make a move?"

"No. It was complicated to start with, but then he had a thing for a friend of mine, and I had to watch from the sidelines as things didn't pan out well."

I draw my brows together, using more brainpower than I have at the moment. "Should I kick his ass? What guy wouldn't want to date you?"

Realization hits me hard as she stares at me through her lashes.

How could I have been so blind?

Yeah, she's my friend's twin sister, but I've never seen her for the woman she is.

I tuck a piece of hair behind her ear. Kendra looks up with hopeful eyes, enticing me to take the next step.

Without another thought, I grip the back of her neck and crash my mouth onto hers, begging and pleading for entrance. She easily grants me access, kissing me back with the same ferocity.

Fuck, she tastes so sweet. But I don't want to do this out here.

Kendra has the same thought as she walks us over to the suite I'm sharing with her brother.

Shit. Bryce.

No, I can't do this.

"Please?" *she says quietly, reading my thoughts.* "I don't want to be alone tonight, and I don't think you do either."

With her hand running down my chest, I grip her hips and drag her inside my room.

I was already harboring quite a bit of guilt for hurting Luke and Gia. Now, as I stare at Kendra's beautiful smile before turning my attention to her brother, a new form of guilt takes its place.

Her crestfallen face the morning after nearly killed me when I said we made a mistake. But I won't hurt another friend by getting involved in a romantic relationship with someone I'm not supposed to.

I won't let history repeat itself, even if I can finally see what's been in front of me this whole time.

Acknowledgements

To my husband, thank you for continuing support and love, for pushing me to do better, and for being proud of me no matter what.

Kate, my soul sister, I don't know what I'd do with you. Seriously. Thank you for being my adult, pushing me throughout this entire process, answering my incessant questions, designing this amazing cover and all the teasers, and keeping me on track with everything I need and don't want to do. Your *Jordie* loves you.

Stacy, my boo, I don't know what I'd do without you. Your belief in my abilities amazes me most days and your unwavering friendship and sisterhood is everything. I love you more than words can express.

Ellie, I'm so glad you took a chance on me. You're the best in the business and I can't thank you enough for everything you do.

Stacey, one of these days, we are going to sit down and drink wine together. Promise.

To all my friends and family who give me all their love and support as I bombard them with messages or ignore them because I'm in the middle of a thought and can't be disturbed, I love you more than I could possibly put into words.

To you, the readers, I'm beyond grateful that you're here, reading my stories, loving them as much as I do. I'm humbled and awestruck with each message and review. Thank you, thank you, thank you. From the bottom of my heart. I'm blessed beyond words.

Sign-up for my newsletter for exclusive excerpts, sneak peeks,
and important information:
http://eepurl.com/cVnX4z

ABOUT
The Author

Jodie Larson is a wife and mother to four beautiful girls, making their home in northern Minnesota along the shore of Lake Superior. When she isn't running around to various activities or working her regular job, you can find her sitting in her favorite spot reading her new favorite book or camped out somewhere quiet trying to write her next manuscript. She's addicted to reading (just ask her kids or husband) and loves talking books even more so with her friends. She's also a lover of all things romance and happily ever after's, whether in movies or in books, as shown in her extensive collection of both.

OTHER BOOKS WRITTEN BY
JODIE LARSON

Available on Amazon and for free on Kindle Unlimited

The Fated Duet
Fated to be Yours (Fated, book 1)
Fated to be Mine (Fated, book 2)

The Lecara Duet
Her Royal Fling (Lecara, book 1)
His Royal Plan (Lecara, book 2)

Lightning Strikes Series
Serenading the Shadows (Lightning Strikes, book 1)
Notes of the Past (Lightning Strikes, book 2)
Forbidden Lyrics (Lightning Strikes, book 3)
Downbeat (Lightning Strikes, book 4)
Little Lullaby (Lightning Strikes, book 5)

Standalones
Lessons of the Heart
I Don't Regret You

You can find Jodie at:

Facebook: www.facebook.com/jodielarsonauthor
Twitter: www.twitter.com/jlarsonauthor
Instagram: www.instagram.com/jodielarson
Website: www.jodielarson.com

Join my reader group to stay up-to-date and get exclusive sneak peeks, giveaways, and more!
http://bit.ly/larsonslovelies

Printed in Great Britain
by Amazon

16723837R00135